# Noémi - A Story of Rock-Dwellers by Sabine Baring-Gould

Sabine Baring-Gould was born on January 28th, 1834. The family had its own manor house at Lew Trenchard on a three-thousand-acre estate, in Devon, England,

His bibliography is immense. 1200 items at a minimum including the hymns 'Onward Christian Soldiers' and 'Now the Day Is Over'.

The family spent much of his childhood travelling in Europe and he was educated mainly by private tutors although he spent two years King's College School in London and a few months at Warwick Grammar School. Here he contracted a bronchial disease that was to plague him throughout his life.

In 1852 he gained entrance to Cambridge University, earning a Bachelor of Arts in 1857, and then a Master of Arts in 1860 from Clare College, Cambridge.

As early as 1853 he had decided to become ordained. In 1864, after his education and several years teaching, he took Holy Orders.

He became the curate at Horbury Bridge in West Riding. Here he met Grace Taylor, the daughter of a mill hand, aged fourteen. During the next few years they fell in love. His vicar, John Sharp, arranged for Grace to live with relatives in York to learn middle-class manners. Baring-Gould, meanwhile, relocated to become perpetual curate at Dalton, near Thirsk.

He and Grace were married in 1868 at Wakefield. Their marriage lasted until her death 48 years later, and the couple had 15 children.

Baring-Gould became the rector of East Mersea in Essex in 1871. In 1872 his father died and he inherited the family estates which included the gift of the living of Lew Trenchard parish. Upon its vacancy in 1881, he took the post, becoming parson as well as squire.

He wrote many novels, his usual writing position was whilst standing, including The Broom-Squire set in the Devil's Punch Bowl (1896), Mehalah and Guavas, the Tinner (1897), a collection of ghost stories, and a 16-volume The Lives of the Saints.

His studies in folklore resulted in The Book of Were-Wolves (1865), a frequently cited study of lycanthropy.

The popular work Curious Myths of the Middle Ages, published in two parts, in 1866 and 1868. Each of the book's twenty-four chapters deals with one medieval superstition, its variants and history.

Grace died in 1916. He had carved on her headstone: Dimidium Animae Meae ("Half my Soul").

Sabine Baring-Gould died on January 2nd, 1924 at Lew Trenchard. He was buried next to Grace.

## Index of Contents

## CHAPTER I

### THE STAIR PERILOUS

Jean Del' Peyra was standing scraping a staff to form a lance-shaft. The sun shone hot upon him, and at his feet lay his shadow as a blot.

He was too much engrossed in his work to lcok about him, till he heard a voice call from somewhere above his head—

"Out of the way, clown!"

Then there crashed down by him a log of wood that rolled to his feet and was followed by another piece.

Now only did Jean look up, and what he saw made him drop his half-finished shaft and forget it. What Jean saw was this: a girl at some distance above him on the face of the rock, swaying a long-handled hammer, with which she was striking at, and dislodging, the steps by which she had ascended, and by means of which alone could she return.

The cliff was of white limestone, or rather chalk, not such as Dover headlands are composed of, and which have given their name to Albion, but infinitely more compact and hard, though scarcely less white. The appearance of the stone was that of fine-grained white limestone. A modern geologist peering among its fossils would say it was chalk. But the period of this tale far antedates the hatching out of the first geologist.

The cliff was that of La Roque Gageac, that shoots up from the Dordogne to the height of four hundred and sixty feet above the river. The lower portion is, however, not perpendicular; it consists of a series of ledges and rapid inclines, on which stands clustered, clinging to the rock, the town of Gageac. But two thirds of the height is not merely a sheer precipice, it overhangs. Half-way up this sheer precipice the weather has gnawed into the rock, where was a bed of softer stone, forming a horizontal cavern, open to the wind and rain, with a roof extending some forty feet, unsupported, above the hard bed that served as floor.

At some time unknown a stair had been contrived in the face of the rock, to reach this terrace a hundred feet above the roofs of the houses below; and then a castle had been built in the cave, consisting of towers and guard-rooms, halls and kitchens; a well had been sunk in the heart of the mountain, and this impregnable fastness had been made into a habitation for man.

It could be reached in but one way, by the stair from below. It could not be reached from above, for the rock overhung the castle walls.

But the stair itself was a perilous path, and its construction a work of ingenuity. To make the position— the eagle nest in the rock—absolutely inaccessible to an enemy, the stair had been contrived so that it could be wrecked by those flying up it, with facility, and that thereby they might cut off possibility of pursuit.

The method adopted was this.

Holes had been bored into the rock-face in gradual ascent from the platform at the foot of the rock to the gate-tower of the castle, nestled on the platform in the precipice. In each such hole a balk or billet of wood was planted, sliced away below where it entered, and this end was then made fast by a wedge driven in under it. From each step, when once secured, that above it could next be made firm. To release the steps a tap from underneath sufficed to loosen the wedge and send it and the balk it supported clattering down.

And now the girl was striking away these steps. What was her purpose? Had she considered what she was doing? To destroy the means of ascent was easy enough; to replace it a labour exacting time and patience. Was she a fool? was she mad?

There was some method in her madness, for she had not knocked away a succession of steps, but two only, with one left in position between.

"'Ware, fool!"

And down the face of the rock and clattering to his feet fell a third.

This was too much.

Jean ran to the foot of the stair and hastened up it till he reached the gap. Further he could not proceed—a step had been dislodged; the next remained intact. Then came another break, a second step in place, and then the third break. Above that stood the girl, swinging the long-handled mallet with which she had loosened the wedges and struck down the steps they held up. She was a handsome girl with dusky skin, but warm with blood under it, dark loose hair, and large deep brown eyes. She stood, athletic, graceful, poised on her stage, swaying the hammer, looking defiantly, insolently, at the youth, with lips half open and pouting.

"Do you know what you are about, madcap?" said he.

"Perfectly. Making you keep your distance, fool."

"Keep distance!" said the youth. "I had no thought of you. I was not pursuing you—I did not know you were here!"

"And now I have woke you to see me."

"What of that? You had acted like a mad thing. I cannot help you, I cannot leap to you. Nothing would make me do so."

"Nothing? Not if I said, 'Come, assist me down'?"

"I could not leap the space. See you—if one step only were thrown down I might venture, but not when every alternate one between us is missing. To leap up were to ensure my fall at the next gap."

"I do not need your help. I can descend. I can spring from one step to the next over the gaps."

"And risk a fall and a broken neck?"

"Then there is one madcap the less in this world."

"For what have you done this?"

"A prank."

"A prank! Yes; but to replace the steps takes time and pains."

"I shall expend neither on them."

"It will give trouble to others."

"If it amuses me, what care I?"

The young man looked at the strange girl with perplexity.

"If every peg of wood were away," said she, "I could yet descend."

"How? Are you a bird—can you fly? Not a cat, not a squirrel could run up or down this rock."

"Fool! I should slip down by the rope. Do you not know that there is a windlass? Do you suppose they take their kegs of wine, their meat, their bread, their fuel up this spider stair? I tell you that there is a rope, and at the end of it a bar of wood. They let this down and bring up what they want affixed to the bar. At pleasure, any man may go up or down that way. Do you not see? It must be so. If they were fast and all the ladders were gone, how should they ever descend? Why, they could not mend the stairs from aloft. It must be done step by step from below. Do you see that, fool?"

"I see that perfectly."

"Very well; I have but to run up, make love to the custodian, and he would swing me down. There; it is easy done!"

"You had best cast down the hammer and let me replace the steps."

"I'll come down without them and without a rope. I can leap. If I cannot creep up as a cat, I can spring down like one—aye! and like a squirrel, too, from one lodging place to another. Stand back and see me."

"Stay!" said Jean. "Why run the risk when not needed?"

"Because I like the risk—it is pepper and mustard to my meat of life. Stand back, clown, or I will spring and strike you over—and down you go and crack your foolish pate."

"If I go—you go also—do you not see that?"

"Look aloft!" said the girl. "Up in that nest—whenever the English are about, up goes into it the Bishop of Sarlat and he takes with him all his treasure, his gold cups and patens, his shrines for holy bones all set with gems, and his bags of coin. There he sits like an old grey owl, Towhit! towhoo—towhit! towhoo! and he looks out this way, that—to see where houses are burning and smoke rises, and when at night the whole world is besprent with red fires—as the sky is with stars, where farms and homesteads are burning. And he says 'Towhit! towhoo! I have my cups and my patens and my coin-bags, and my dear little holy bones, all safe here. Towhit! towhoo! And best of all—I am safe—my unholy old bones also, whoo! whoo! whoo! Nobody can touch me—whoo! whoo! whoo!'"

"Is he there now?"

"No, he is not. There is no immediate danger. Only a few as guard, that is all. If I were a man, I'd take the place and smoke the old owl out, and rob him of his plunder. I'd keep the shrines, and throw the holy rubbish away!"

"How would you do that?"

"I have been considering. I'd be let down over the edge of the cliff and throw in fireballs, till I had set the castle blazing."

"And then?"

"Then I'd have grappling-irons and crook them to the walls, and swing in under the ledge, and leap on the top of the battlements, and the place would fall. I'd cast the old bishop out if he would not go, and carry off all his cups and shrines and coin."

"It would be sacrilege!"

"Bah! What care I?" Then, after enjoying the astonishment of the lad, she said: "With two or three bold spirits it might be done. Will you join me? Be my mate, and we will divide the plunder." She burst into a merry laugh. "It would be sport to smoke out the old owl and send him flying down through the air, blinking and towhooing, to break his wings, or his neck, or his crown there—on those stones below."

"I'm not English—I'm no brigand!" answered the young man vehemently.

"I'm English!" said the girl.

"What? An English woman or devil?"

"I'm English—I'm Gascon. I'm anything where there is diversion to be got and plunder to be obtained. Oh, but we live in good times! Deliver me from others where there is nothing doing, no sport, no chevauchee no spoil, no fighting."

Then suddenly she threw away the hammer and spread her arms as might a bird preparing to fly, bent her lithe form as might a cricket to leap.

"Stand aside! Go back! 'Ware, I am coming!"

The lad hastily beat a retreat down the steps. He could do no other. Each step was but two feet in length from the rock. There was no handrail; no two persons could pass on it. Moreover, the impetus of the girl, if she leaped from one foothold to the next, and the next, and then again to the stair where undamaged, would be prodigious; she would require the way clear that she might descend bounding, swinging down the steep flight, two stages at a leap, till she reached the bottom. An obstruction would be fatal to her, and fatal to him who stood in her way.

No word of caution, no dissuasion was of avail. In her attitude, in the flash of her eyes, in the tone of her voice, in the thrill that went through her agile frame, Jean saw that the leap was inevitable. He therefore hastened to descend, and when he reached the bottom, turned to see her bound.

He held his breath. The blood in his arteries stood still. He set his teeth, and all the muscles of his body contracted as with the cramp.

He saw her leap.

Once started, nothing could arrest her.

On her left hand was the smooth face of the rock, without even a blade of grass, a harebell, a tuft of juniper growing out of it. On her right was void. If she tripped, if she missed her perch, if she miscalculated her weight, if she lost confidence for one instant, if her nerve gave way in the slightest, if she was not true of eye, nimble of foot, certain in judging distance, then she would shoot down just as had the logs she had cast below.

As certainly as he saw her fall would Jean spring forward in the vain hope of breaking her fall, as certainly to be struck down and perish with her.

One—a whirl before his eyes. As well calculate her leaps as count the spokes in a wheel as it revolves on the road.

One—two—three—thirty—a thousand—nothing!

"There, clown!"

She was at the bottom, her hands extended, her face flushed with excitement and pleasure.

"You see—what I can dare and do."

## CHAPTER II

## WHO IS THE FOOL NOW?

There boiled up in the youth's heart a feeling of wrath and indignation against the girl who in sheer wantonness had imperiled her life and had given to him a moment of spasm of apprehension.

Looking full into her glittering brown eyes, he said—

"You have cast at me ill names. I have been to you but clown and fool; I have done nothing to merit such titles; I should never have thrown a thought away on you, but have gone on scraping my shaft, had not you done a silly thing—a silly thing. Acted like a fool, and a fool only!"

"You dare not do what I have done."

"If there be a need I will do it. If I do it for a purpose there is no folly in it. That is folly where there is recklessness for no purpose."

"I had a purpose!"

"A purpose?—what? To call my attention to you, to make me admire your daring, all to no end. Or was it in mere inconsiderate prank? A man is not brave merely because he is so stupid that he does not see the consequences before him. A blind man may walk where I should shrink from treading. And stupidity blinds some eyes that they run into danger and neither see nor care for the danger or for the consequences that will ensue on their rashness."

The girl flushed with anger.

"I am not accustomed to be spoken to thus," she said, and stamped her foot on the pavement of the platform.

"All the better for you that it is spoken at last."

"And who are you that dare say it?"

"I—I am Jean del' Peyra."

The girl laughed contemptuously. "I never heard the name."

"I have told you my name, what is yours?" asked the boy, and he picked up his staff and began once more to point it.

There was indifference in his tone, indifference in the act, that exasperated the girl.

"You do not care—I will not say."

"No," he answered, scraping leisurely at the wood. "I do not greatly care. Why should I? You have shown me to-day that you do not value yourself, and you do not suppose, then, that I can esteem one who does not esteem herself."

"You dare say that!" The girl flared into fury. She stooped to pick up the hammer. Jean put his foot on it.

"No," said he. "You would use that, I suppose, to knock out my brains, because I show you no homage, because I say that you have acted as a fool, that your bravery is that of a fool, that your thoughts—aye, your thoughts of plunder and murder against the Bishop of Sarlat, your old owl—towhit, towhoo! are the thoughts of a fool. No—I do not care for the name of a fool."

"Why did you run up the steps? Why did you cry to me to desist from knocking out the posts? Why concern yourself a mite about me, if you so despise me?" gasped the girl, and it seemed as though the words shot like flames from her lips.

"Because we are of like blood—that is all!" answered Jean, coolly.

"Like blood! Hear him—hear him! He and I—he—he and I of like blood, and he a del' Peyra! And I—I am a Noémi!"

"So—Noémi! That is your name?"

"And I," continued the girl in her raging wrath, "I—learn this—I am the child of Le Gros Guillem. Have you ever heard of the Gros Guillem?" she asked in a tone of triumph, like the blast of a victor's trumpet.

Jean lowered his staff, and looked steadily at her. His brows were contracted, his lips were set firm.

"So!" he said, after a pause. "The daughter of Gros Guillem?"

"Aye—have you heard of him?"

"Of course I have heard of him."

"And of the del' Peyras who ever heard?" asked the girl with mockery and scorn, and snapped her fingers.

"No—God be thanked!—of the del' Peyras you have never heard as of the Gros Guillem."

"The grapes—the grapes are sour!" scoffed the girl.

"I wonder at nothing you have done," said the boy sternly, "since you have told me whence you come. Of the thorn—thorns; of the nettle—stings; of the thistle—thistles—all after their kind. No! God be praised!" The boy took off his cap and looked up. "The Gros Guillem and my father, Ogier del' Peyra, are not to be spoken of in one sentence here, nor will be from the White Throne on the Day of Doom."

Looking steadily at the girl seething with anger, with mortified pride, and with desire to exasperate him, he said—

"I should never have thought that you sprang from the Gros Guillem. The likeness must be in the heart, it is not in the face."

"Have you seen my father?" asked the girl.

"I have never seen him, but I have heard of him."

"What have you heard?"

"That he is very tall and spider-like in build; they call him 'le gros' in jest, for he is not stout, but very meagre. He has long hands and feet, and a long head with red hair, and pale face with sunspots, and very faint blue eyes, under thick red brows. That is what I am told Le Gros Guillem is like. But you—"

"Describe me—go on!"

"No!" answered Jean. "There is no need. You see yourself every day in the glass. When there is no glass you look at yourself in the water; when no water, you look at yourself in your nails."

"When there is no water, I look at myself in your eyes, and see a little brown creature there—that is me. Allons!"

She began to laugh. Much of her bad temper had flown; she was a girl of rapidly changing moods.

It was true that she was mirrored in Jean del' Peyra's eyes. He was observing her attentively. Never before had he seen so handsome a girl, with olive, transparent skin, through which the flush of colour ran like summer lightning in a summer cloud—such red lips, such rounded cheek and chin; such an easy, graceful figure! The magnificent burnished black hair was loose and flowing over her shoulders; and her eyes!—they had the fire of ten thousand flints lurking in them and flashing out at a word.

"How come you here?" asked Jean, in a voice less hard and in a tone less indifferent than before. "This place, La Roque Gageac, is not one for a daughter of Le Gros Guillem. Here we are French. At Domme they are English, and that is the place for your father."

"Ah!" said the girl in reply, "among us women French or English are all the same. We are both and we are neither. I suppose you are French?"

"Yes, I am French."

"And a Bishop's man?"

"I live on our own land—Del Peyraland, at Ste. Soure."

"And I am with my aunt here. My father considers Domme a little too rough a place for a girl. He has sent me hither. At the gates they did not ask me if I were French or English. They let me through, but not my father's men. They had to ride back to Domme."

"He cannot come and see you here?"

The girl laughed. "If he were to venture here, they would hang him—not give him half an hour to make his peace with Heaven!—hang him—hang him as a dog!"

"So!—and you are even proud of such a father!"

"So!—and even I am proud to belong to one whose name is known. I thank my good star I do not belong to a nobody of whom none talk, even as an Ogier del' Peyra."

"You are proud of your father—of Le Gros Guillem!" exclaimed Jean; and now his brow flushed with anger, and his eye sparkled. "Proud of that routier and rouffien, who is the scourge, the curse of the country round! Proud of the man that has desolated our land, has made happy wives into wailing widows, and glad children into despairing orphans; who has wrecked churches, and drunk— blaspheming God at the time—out of the gold chalices; who has driven his sword into the bowels of his own Mother Country, and has scorched her beautiful face with his firebrands! I know of Le Gros Guillem—who does not?—know of him by the curses that are raised by his ill deeds, the hatred he has sown, the vows of vengeance that are registered—"

"Which he laughs at," interrupted Noémi.

"Which he laughs at now," pursued the boy angrily, and anger gave fluency to his tongue. "But do you not suppose that a day of reckoning will arrive? Is Heaven deaf to the cries of the sufferers? Is Humanity all-enduring, and never likely to revolt—and, when she does, to exact a terrible revenge? The labourer asks for naught but to plough his land in peace, the merchant nothing but to be allowed to go on his journey unmolested, the priest has no higher desire than to say his Mass in tranquillity. And all this might be but for Le Gros Guillem and the like of him. Let the English keep their cities and their provinces; they belong to them by right. But is Le Gros Guillem English? Was Perducat d'Albret English? What of Le petit Mesquin? of the Archpriest? of Cervolle? Were they English? Are those real English faces that we fear and hate? Are they not the faces of our own countrymen, who call themselves English, that they may plunder and murder their fellow-countrymen and soak with blood and blast with fire the soil that reared them?"

Noémi was somewhat awed by his vehemence, but she said—

"Rather something to be talked about than a nothing at all."

"Wrong, utterly wrong!" said Jean. "Rather be the storm that bursts and wrecks all things than be still beneficent Nature in her order which brings to perfection? Any fool can destroy; it takes a wise man to build up. You—you fair and gay young spirit, tell me have you ever seen that of which you speak so lightly, of which you jest as if it were a matter of pastime? Have you gone tripping after your father, treading in his bloody footprints, holding up your skirts lest they should touch the festering carcases on either side the path he has trod?"

"No," answered the girl, and some of the colour went out of her face, leaving it the finest, purest olive in tint.

"Then say no more about your wish to have a name as a routier and to be the terror of the countryside, till you have experienced what it is that terrorises the land."

"One must live," said Noémi.

"One may live by helping others to live—as does the peasant, and the artisan, as the merchant; or by destroying the life of others—as does the routier and the vulgar robber," answered Jean.

Then Noémi caught his wrist and drew him aside under an archway. Her quick eye had seen the castellar coming that way; he had not been in the castle in the face of the rock, but in the town; and he was now on his way back. He would find the means of ascent broken, and must repair it before reaching his eyrie.

"Who is the fool now?" said Jean del' Peyra. "You, who were knocking away the steps below you, calculating that if you destroyed that stair, you could still descend by the custodian's rope and windlass. See—he was not there. You would have been fast as a prisoner till the ladder was restored; and small bones would have been made of you, Gros Guillem's daughter, for playing such a prank as that!"

Unseen they watched the man storming, swearing, angrily gathering up the pegs and wedges and the hammer, and ascending the riskful flight of steps to replace the missing pieces of wood in their sockets, and peg them firmly and sustainingly with their wedges.

"What you did in your thoughtlessness, that your father and the like of him do in their viciousness, and do on a grander scale," said Jean. "They are knocking away the pegs in the great human ladder, destroying the sower with his harvest, the merchant with his trade, the mason, the carpenter, the weaver with their crafts, the scholar with his learning, the man of God with his lessons of peace and goodwill. And at last Le Gros Guillem and such as he will be left alone, above a ruined world on the wreckage of which he has mounted, to starve, when there is nothing more to be got, because the honest getters have all been struck down. Who is the fool now?"

"Have done!" said the girl impatiently. "You have moralised enough—you should be a clerk!"

"We are all made moralists when we see honesty trampled under foot. Well for you, Noémi, with your light head and bad heart—"

"My bad heart!"

"Aye, your bad heart. Well for you that you are a harmless girl and not a boy, or you would have followed quick in your father's steps and built yourself up as hateful a name."

"I, a harmless girl?"

"Yes, a harmless girl. Your hands are feeble, and however malicious your heart, you can do none a mischief, save your own self."

"You are sure of that?"

"Mercifully it is so. The will to hurt and ruin may be present, but you are weak and powerless to do the harm you would."

"Is a woman so powerless?"

"Certainly."

She ran up a couple of steps, caught him by the shoulders, stooped, and kissed him on the lips, before he was aware what she was about to do.

"Say that again! A woman is weak! A woman cannot ravage and burn, and madden and wound—not with a sword and a firebrand, but—"

She stooped. The boy was bewildered—his pulses leaping, his eye on fire, his head reeling. She kissed him again.

"These are her weapons!" said Noémi. "Who is the fool now?"


CHAPTER III

THE WOLVES OUT

Jean Del' Peyra was riding home, a distance of some fifteen miles from La Roque Gageac. His way led through forests of oak clothing the slopes and plateau of chalk. The road was bad—to be more exact, there was no road; there was but a track.

In times of civil broil, when the roads were beset by brigands, travellers formed or found ways for themselves through the bush, over the waste land, away from the old and neglected arteries of traffic. The highways were no longer kept up—there was no one to maintain them in repair, and if they were sound no one would travel on them who could avoid them by a détour, when exposed to be waylaid, plundered carried off to a dungeon, and put to ransom.

To understand the condition of affairs, a brief sketch of the English domination in Guyenne is necessary.

By the marriage of Eleanor, daughter and heiress of William X., Earl of Poitou and Duke of Aquitaine, with Henry of Anjou, afterwards Henry II. of England, in 1152, the vast possessions of her family were united to those of the Angevin house, which claimed the English crown.

By this union the house of Anjou suddenly rose to be a power, superior to that of the French crown on the Gaulish soil, which it cut off entirely from the mouths of the Seine and the Loire, and nipped between its Norman and Aquitanian fingers. The natives of the South—speaking their own language, of different race, aspirations, character, from those in the North—had no traditional attachment to the French throne, and no ideal of national concentration about it into one great unity. Here and there, dotted about as islets in the midst of the English possessions in the South, were feudal or ecclesiastical baronies, or townships, that were subject immediately to the French crown, and exempt from allegiance to the English King; and these acted as germs, fermenting in the country, and gradually but surely influencing the minds of all, and drawing all to the thought that for the good of the land it were better that it should belong to France than to England. Such was the diocese and county of Sarlat. This had belonged to a monastic church founded in the eighth century, but it had been raised to an episcopal see in 1317, and had never wavered in its adherence to the French interest. Sarlat was not on the Dordogne, but lay buried, concealed in the depths of oak-woods, accessible only along narrow defiles commanded at every point by rocky headlands; and the key to the episcopal city was La Roque Gageac, the impregnable fortress and town on the pellucid, rippling Dordogne—the town cramped to the steep slope, the castle nestling into an excavation in the face of the abrupt scarp.

Nearly opposite La Roque stood an insulated block of chalk, with precipices on all sides, and to secure this, in 1280, Philip III. of France built on it a free town, exempt from all taxes save a trifling house-charge due to himself; which town he hoped would become a great commercial centre, and a focus whence French influence might radiate to the south of the Dordogne. Unhappily the importance of Domme made it a prize to be coveted by the English, and in 1347 they took it. They were expelled in 1369, but John Chandos laid siege to it in 1380 and took it again, and from that date it remained uninterruptedly in their hands till the end of the English power in Aquitaine. For three hundred years had Guyenne pertained to the English crown, many of the towns and most of the nobility had no aspirations beyond serving the Leopards. The common people were supremely indifferent whether the Fleur-de-lys or the Leopards waved above them, so long as they were left undisturbed. It was precisely because they had not the boon of tranquillity afforded them by subjection to the English that they turned at last with a sigh of despair to the French. But it was to the Leopards, the hereditary coat of Guyenne, that they looked first, and it was only when the Leopard devoured them that they inclined to the Lilies.

The reason for this general dissatisfaction and alienation was the violence of the nobility, and the freebooters, who professed to act for the Crown of England, and to have patents warranting them to act licentiously. These men, caring only for their own interests, doing nothing to advance the prosperity of the land, used their position, their power, to undermine and ruin it. They attacked the towns whether under the English or French allegiance—that mattered nothing—and forced the corporations to enter into compacts with them, whereby they undertook to pay them an annual subvention, not to ensure protection, but merely to escape pillage. But even these patis, as they were called, were precarious, and did not cover a multitude of excuses for infringement of the peace. If, for instance, a merchant of Sarlat was in debt to a man of Domme, the latter appealed to his feudal master, who, in spite of any patis granted, swooped down on such members of the community of Sarlat as he could lay hold of, and held them in durance till not only was the debt paid, but he was himself indemnified for the trouble he had taken in obtaining its discharge.

If these things were done in the green tree, what in the dry?

In addition to the feudal seigneurs in their castles, ruling over their seigneuries, and nominally amenable to the English crown, there were the routiers, captains of free companies, younger sons of noble houses, bastards, runaway prisoners: any idle and vicious rascal who could collect thirty men of like kidney constituted himself a captain, made for himself and his men a habitation by boring into the limestone or chalk rock, in an inaccessible position, whence he came down at pleasure and ravaged and robbed, burned and murdered indiscriminately, the lands and houses and persons of those, whether French or English, who had anything to attract his greed, or who had incurred his resentment.

When Arnaud Amanieu, Sire d'Albret, transferred his allegiance from the English King to the King of France, he was seen by Froissart in Paris, sad of countenance, and he gave this as his reason: "Thank God! I am well in health, but my purse was fuller when I warred on behalf of the King of England. Then when we rode on adventures, there were always some rich merchants of Toulouse, of Condom, of La Réole, or Bergerac for us to squeeze. Every day we got some spoil to stuff our superfluities and jollities— alack! now all is dead and dull." That was the saying of a great Prince, whom the King of France delighted to honour. Now hear the words of a common routier: "How rejoiced were we when we rode abroad and captured many a rich prior or merchant, or a train of mules laden with Brussels cloths, or furs from the fair of Landit, or spices from Bruges, or silks from Damascus! All was ours, and we ransomed men at our good pleasure. Every day fresh spoil. The villages purveyed to us, and the rustics brought us corn, flour, bread, litter, wines, meat, and fowl; we were waited on as kings, we were clothed as princes, and when we rode abroad the earth quaked before us."

In this terrible time agriculture languished, trade was at a standstill. Bells were forbidden to be rung in churches from vespers till full day, lest they should direct the freebooters to villages that they might ravage. The towns fortified themselves, the villagers converted their churches into castles, and surrounded them with moats. Children were planted on all high points to keep watch, and give warning at the flash of a helmet. Wretched peasants spent their nights in islands in mid-river or in caves underground.

No one who has not visited the country swept and re-swept by these marauders can have any conception of the agony through which the country passed. It is furrowed, torn, to the present day by the picks of the ruffians who sought for themselves nests whence they might survey the land and swoop down on it, but above all by the efforts of the tortured to hide themselves—here burrowing underground like moles in mid-field, there boring out chambers in clefts of the rock, there constructing for themselves cabins in the midst of mosquito-haunted marshes, and there, again, ensconcing themselves in profound depths of trackless forests.

As Jean del' Peyra rode along, he shook his head and passed his hand over his face, as though to free it from cobwebs that had gathered about his eyes and were irritating him. But these were no spider-threads: what teased and confused him were other fibres, spun by that brown witch, Noémi.

He was angry, indignant with her, but his anger and indignation were, as it were, trowel and prong that dug and forked the thoughts of her deep into his mind. He thought of her standing before him, quivering with wrath, the fire flashing and changing hue in her opalescent brown eyes, and the hectic flame running through her veins and tinging cheek and brow. He thought of her voice, so full of tone, so flexible, as opalescent in melodious change as her eyes iridescent of light.

That she—she with such a smooth face, such slim fingers—should talk of crime as a joke, exult over the misery of her fellows! A very leopard in litheness and in beauty, and a very leopard in heart.

Jean del' Peyra's way led down the head stream of the Lesser Beune. The valley was broad—one level marsh—and, in the evening, herons were quivering in it, stooping to pick up an eft or a young roach.

"Ah! you vile creature!" sang forth Jean, as a black hare rose on his left and darted past him into the wood. "Prophet of evil! But what else in these untoward times and in this evil world can one expect but omens of ill?"

The track by which Jean descended emerged from the dense woods upon open ground. As the Beune slid to a lower level, it passed under precipices of rock, about a hundred or a hundred and fifty feet high; and these cliffs, composed of beds of various softness, were horizontally channelled, constituting terraces, each terrace unsupported below, or rather thrown forward over a vault. Moreover, there was not one of these platforms of rock that was not tenanted. In the evening, peasants returning from their work were ascending to their quarters by scrambling up the rocks where vertical, by means of notches cut in the stone, into which they thrust their hands and feet. Where the ledges overhung, the men were drawn up by ropes to the platforms above.

But not only was this the case with men, but with their oxen. Jean passed and saluted a farmer who was in process of placing his beasts in a position of security for the night. His wife was above, in the rock, and was working a windlass by means of which an ox was being gradually lifted from the ground by broad bands passed under its belly, and so was raised to the height of some thirty feet, where the beast, accustomed to this proceeding, quickly stepped on to a narrow path cut in the rock, and walked to its stable, also rock-hewn in the face of the cliff.

In another place was a woman with her children closing up the opening of a grotto that was level with the soil. This was effected by a board which fitted into a rebate in the rock, and then the woman, after putting her children within, heaped stones and sods against the board to disguise it; and when this had been done to her satisfaction, she crawled in by a hole that had been left for the purpose, and by a cord pulled after her a bunch of brambles that served to plug and disguise this hole.

Bitterness welled up in the heart of Jean as he noticed all these efforts made by the poor creatures to place themselves in security during the hours of darkness.

"Ah, Fontaineya!" called Jean to the farmer who was superintending the elevation of his second ox. "How goes the world with you?"

"Bad, but might be worse—even as with you."

"With me things are not ill."

"Whence come you, then?"

"From La Roque."

"Aha! Not from Ste. Soure?"

"No, I have been from home these fourteen days."

"Then do not say things are not ill with you till you have been home," remarked the peasant dryly.

"What has happened?" asked Jean, his blood standing still with alarm.

"The wolves have been hunting!"

"What wolves?"

"The red. Le Gros Guillem."

"He has been to Ste. Soure?"

"He has been to where Ste. Soure was."

## CHAPTER IV

IN NOMINE BEELZEBUB

It was strange. The first recoil wave of the shock caused by this tidings broke into foam and fury against Noémi. Jean del' Peyra did not think of his loss, of the ruin of his home, of the sufferings of his people, but of Noémi laughing, making light of these things.

It was strange. Instead of striking spurs into his steed's flank and galloping forward to the scene of desolation, involuntarily, unconsciously, he turned his horse's head round, so that he faced the far-off Gageac, and with set teeth and flashing eye and lowering brow, wiped his lips with the sleeve of his right arm—wiped them not once nor twice, but many times as to wipe off and wipe away for ever the sensation, the taint, the fire that had been kindled there by the kisses he had received.

Then only did he wheel his horse about and gallop—where galloping was possible—down the valley of the Beune. The Beune is a stream rather than a river, that flows into the Vézère. It has a singular quality: so charged are the waters with lime that they petrify, or rather encrust, the roots of all plants growing in the morass through which they flow, by this means forming dams for itself, which it gradually surmounts to form others. The original bottom of the ravine must be at a considerable depth under the flat marsh of living and dead waterweed, of active and paralysed marsh plants, of growing and petrified moss that encumbers it, and extends to the very faces of the rocks.

At the present day a road laboriously constructed, and where it crossed the valley perpetually sinking and perpetually renovated, gives access to the springs of the Beune. It was not so in the fifteenth century. Then a track lay along the sides where the ground was solid—that is to say, where it consisted of rubble from the hill-sides; but where the marsh reached the abrupt walls of cliff, there the track clambered up the side of the valley, and surmounted the escarpments.

Consequently progress in former ages in that part was not as facile as it is at present.

Jean was constrained speedily to relax the pace at which he was proceeding.

As long as he was in forest and rough place he was secure: the brigands did not care to penetrate, at all events at nightfall, into out-of-the-way places, and where they might fall into ambuscades.

It was otherwise when he came to where the Beune distilled from its sponge of moss into the rapidly flowing Vézère. Here was a great amphitheatre of scarped sides of rock, all more or less honeycombed with habitations and refuges.

Here, on his left-hand side, looking north, scowling over the pleasant and smiling basin of the Vézère, was the castle of the Great Guillem. It consisted of a range of caves or overhanging ledges of rock, the faces of which had been built up with walls, windows, and crenelations, and a gate-house had been constructed to command the only thread of a path by which the stronghold could be reached.

From this castle watch was kept, and no one could ascend or descend the valley unobserved. Jean was on the same bank as the fortress of Guillem, though considerably above it. He must cross the river, and to do this, ascend it to the ford.

He moved along carefully and watchfully. The dusk of evening concealed his movements, and he was able, unnoticed, or at all events unmolested, to traverse the Vézère and pass on the further side of the river down stream, in face of the strong place of Le Gros Guillem.

A couple of leagues further down was a hamlet, or rather village, called Le Peuch Ste. Soure, clustered at the foot of a cliff or series of cliffs that rose out of a steep incline of rubble. The houses were gathered about a little church dedicated to Ste. Soure. The white crags above were perforated with habitations. A scent of fire was in the air, and in the gloaming Jean could see the twinkle of sparks running, dying out, reappearing where something had been consumed by flames, but was still glowing in places, and sparks were wandering among its ashes. As he drew nearer he heard wailing, and with the wailing voices raised in cursing.

A sickness came on the lad's heart; he knew but too well what this all signified—desolation to many homes, ruin to many families.

"Hold! Who goes?"

"It is I—Jean del' Peyra."

"Well—pass. You will find your father. He is with the Rossignols."

Jean rode on. There were tokens of confusion on all sides. Here a rick was smouldering, and there a house was wrecked, the door broken, and the contents of the dwelling thrown out in the way before it. Pigs that had escaped from their styes ran about rooting after food, and dogs snarled and carried off fragments of meat. A few peasants were creeping about timidly, but, alarmed at the appearance in their midst of a man on horseback, and unable in the dusk to distinguish who he was, they fled to conceal themselves. Jean leaped from his horse, hitched it up, and strode on, with beating heart and bounding pulse, to a house which he knew was that of the Rossignols.

He entered the door. A light shone through the low window. It was characteristic of the times that in every village and hamlet the windows—the only windows—were so turned inwards on a street or yard that they revealed no light at night when a candle was kindled or a fire burned brightly on the hearth, lest the light should betray to a passing marauder the presence of a house which might be looted.

Jean bowed his head and entered at the low door. The fire was flashing in the large open chimney. A bundle of vine faggots had been thrown on, and the light filled the chamber with its orange glare.

By this light Jean saw a bed with a man lying on it; and a woman crying, beating her head and uttering wild words—her children clinging to her, sobbing, frightened, imploring her to desist.

Erect, with a staff in his hand, stood a grey-headed, thick-bearded man, with dark eyes shadowed under heavy brows.

He turned sharply as the lad entered.

"Hah! Jean, you are back. It is well. It is well you were not here this day earlier. If they had taken you, there would have been a heavy ransom to pay, by the Holy Napkin of Cadouin! And how to redeem those already taken I know not."

"What has been done to Rossignol, father?" asked Jean, going to the bed.

"What will be done to the rest unless the ransom be forthcoming in fourteen days. They have left him thus, to show us what will be the fate of the seven others."

"Seven others, father?"

"Aye; they have taken off seven of the men of Ste. Soure. We must find the ransom, or they will send them back to us, even after the fashion of this poor man."

"Is he dead, father?"

The man lying on the bed moved, and, raising himself on his elbow, said—

"Young master, I am worse than dead. Dead, I would be no burden. Living, I shall drag my darlings underground with me."

Then the woman, frantic with grief, turned on her knees, threw up her hands, and uttered a stream of mingled prayer and imprecation—prayer to Heaven and prayer to Hell; to Heaven to blast and torture the destroyers of her house, to Hell to hear her cry if Heaven were deaf. It was not possible for Jean to learn details from her in this fury and paroxysm. He drew his father outside the door and shut it.

"Father," said he, "tell me what has taken place. It was Le Gros Guillem, was it not?"

"Aye, Le Gros Guillem. We did not know he was in his church, we thought he was in Domme, and would be occupied there, and we gave less heed and kept less close watch. You see there were, we knew or supposed, but three men in the church, and so long as they were supplied with food and wine, we had little fear. But we had not reckoned right on Guillem. He came back in the night with a score of men, and they rushed down on us; they crossed the river during the day, when the men were in the fields and about their work, and the women and children alone in the houses. When it was seen that the routiers were coming, then the church bell was rung, but we had little or no time to prepare; they were on us and in every house, breaking up the coffers, sacking the closets."

"Did they get into Le Peuch, father?"

"No; when we heard the bell, then we shut the gates and barricaded; but there were not four men in the castle, myself included. What could we do? We could only look on and witness the destruction; and one of the men in the castle was Limping Gaston, who was no good at all; and another was Blind Bartholomew, who could not see an enemy and distinguish him from a friend. When the men in the fields heard the bell, they came running home, to save what might be saved; but it was too late. The ruffians were there robbing, maltreating, and they took them as they came on—seven of them—and bound their hands behind them, and these they have carried off. They have burned the stack of corn of Jean Grano. The wife of Mussidan was baking. They have carried off all her loaves, and when she entreated them to spare some they swore at another word they would throw one of her babes into the oven. They have ransacked every house, and spoiled what they could not carry away. And the rest of the men, when they saw how those who came near Ste. Soure were taken, fled and hid themselves. Some of the women, carrying their children, came up the steep slope before the routiers arrived, and we received them into the castle; but others remained, hoping to save some of their stuff, and not thinking that the enemy was so nigh. So they were beaten to tell where any money was hidden. The wife of Drax—she has had her soles so cut with vine-rods that she cannot walk; but she was clever—she told where some old Roman coins were hid in a pot, and not where were her silver livres of French money."

"How long were they here?"

"I cannot tell, Jean. It seemed a century. It may have been an hour."

"They have carried off seven men."

"Yes, to Domme, or to the church. I cannot say where. And we must send the ransom in fourteen days, or Le Gros Guillem swears he will return them all to us tied on the backs of mules, treated as he has treated Rossignol. He said he left us Rossignol as a refresher."

"But what has he done to Rossignol?"

"Hamstrung him. He can never walk again. From his thighs down he is powerless—helpless as a babe in arms."

Jean uttered an exclamation of horror.

"Father, there must be an end put to these things! We must rouse the country."

"We must pay the ransom first, or all those poor fellows will be sent back to us like as is Rossignol."

"Let us go into the house," said Jean, and threw open the door. "We must do something for these unhappy creatures."

"Aye," said his father, "and something must be done to save seven other houses from being put in the same condition. Where shall we get the money?"

"We will consider that presently—first to this man."

A strange spectacle met their eyes when they re-entered the house of the Rossignols.

The woman had suspended something dark to a crook in the ceiling, had brought glowing ashes from the hearth, and had placed them in a circle on the floor below this dark object, and had spilled tallow over the red cinders, and the tallow having melted, had become ignited, so that a flicker of blue flame shot about the ring, and now and then sent up a jet of yellow flame like a long tongue that licked the suspended object. The woman held back her children, and in one hand she had a long steel pin or skewer, with a silver head to it, wherewith she had been wont to fasten up her hair. She had withdrawn this from her head, and all her black hair was flowing about her face and shoulders.

"See!" yelled she, and the glitter of her eyes was terrible. "See! it is the heart of Le Gros Guillem. I will punish him for all he has done to me. This for my man's nerves that he has cut." She made a stab with her pin at the suspended object, which Jean and his father now saw was a bullock's heart. "This for all the woe he has brought on me!" She stabbed again. "See, see, my children, how he twists and tosses! Ha! ha! Gros Guillem, am I paining you? Do you turn to escape me? Do I strike spasms of terror into your heart? Ha! ha! the Rossignol is a song-bird, but her beak is sharp."

Jean caught the woman's hand.

"Stand back!" he cried, "this is devilry. This will bring you to the stake."

"What care I—so long as I torture and stab and burn Le Gros Guillem! And who will denounce me for harming him? Will the Church—which he has pillaged? Will you—whom he has robbed? Let me alone—see—see how the flames burn him! Ha! ha! Le Gros Guillem! Am I swinging you! Dance, dance in fire! Swing, swing in anguish! For my children this!" and she stabbed at the heart again.

The woman was mad with despair and hate and terror. Jean stood back, put his hand to his mouth, and said with a groan—

"My God! would Noémi were here!"

"In Nomine Beelzebub!" shrieked the woman, and struck the heart down into the melted flaming fat on the floor.

CHAPTER V

A Heavy sum of money had to be raised, and that within a fortnight.

The Del' Peyra family was far from wealthy. It owned a little seigneurie, Ste. Soure, little else. It took its name from the rocks among which it had its habitation, from the rocks among which its land lay in brown patches, and from which a scanty harvest was reaped. Only in the valley where there was alluvial soil were there pastures for cattle, and on the slopes vineyards whence wine could be expressed. The arable land on the plateaus above the valley of the Vézère was thin and poor enough. A little grain could be grown among the flints and chips of chalk, but it was scanty and poor in quality. If the territories owned by the Del' Peyras had been extensive, then vastness of domain might have compensated for its poor quality. But such was not the case.

The Castle of Le Peuch above Ste. Soure was but small; it consisted of a cluster of buildings leaning against the upright cliff at the summit of a steep incline. This natural glacis of rubble, at an inclination so rapid that the ascent was a matter of difficulty, was in itself a considerable protection to it. The castle could not be captured at a rush, for no rush could be made up a slope which was surmountable only with loss of wind. But supposing the main buildings were stormed, still the inhabitants were sure of escape, for from the roof of the castle they could escalade the precipices to a series of chambers scooped out of the rock, at several successive elevations, each stage being defendable, and only to be surmounted by a ladder. The castle itself was hardly so big as a modern farmhouse. It consisted of but three or four small chambers, one of which served as kitchen and hall. Le Peuch was not a place to stand much of a siege; it was rather what was called in those times a place-forte, a stronghold in which people could take temporary refuge from the freebooters who swept the open country, and had no engines for the destruction of walls, nor time to expend in a regular siege. To the poor at that period, the church-tower was the one hold of security, where they put their chests in which were all their little treasures; and it was one of the bitterest complaints against a rapacious Bishop of Rodez, that he levied a fee for his own pocket on all these cypress and ashen boxes confided to the sanctuary of the parish church. When the signal was given that an enemy was in sight, then men and women crowded to the church and barred its doors. A visitor to the Périgord will this day see many a village church which bears tokens of having been a fortress. The lowest storey is church; the floors above are so contrived as to serve as places of refuge, with all appliances for a residence in them. When Louis VII. was ravaging the territories of his indocile vassal, the Count of Champagne, he set fire to the church of the little town of Vitry, in which all the citizens, their wives and children, had taken refuge, and thirteen hundred persons perished in the flames. Such was war in the Middle Ages. When Henry V. of England was entreated not to burn the towns and villages through which he passed, "Bah!" said he, "would you have me eat my meat without mustard?"

At Ste. Soure there was no church-tower, the place of refuge of the villagers was Le Peuch; but the attack of the marauders had been too sudden and unexpected for them to reach it.

What was to be done? The ransom demanded for the seven men was a hundred livres of Bergerac—that is to say, a sum equivalent at the present time to about one thousand nine hundred pounds. Unless the men were redeemed, the Sieur of Le Peuch would be ruined. No men would remain under his protection when he could neither protect nor deliver them. If he raised the sum, it must be at a ruinous rate, that would impoverish him for years. He was stunned with the magnitude of the disaster. There was but a fortnight in which not only must he resolve what to do, but have the money forthcoming.

After the first stupefaction was over, the old man's heart was full of wrath.

Ogier del' Peyra had been a peaceable man, a good landlord, never oppressing his men, rather dull in head and slow of thought, but right-minded and straightforward. No little seigneur in all the district was so respected. Perhaps it was for this reason that his lands had hitherto been spared by the ravagers. He was not one who had been a hot partisan of the French and a fiery opponent of the English, or rather of those who called themselves English. He had wished for nothing so much as to remain neutral.

But now Le Gros Guillem, who respected nothing and nobody, had suddenly dealt him a staggering blow from which he could hardly recover.

The effect when the first numbness was passed was such as is often the case with dull men, slow to move. Once roused and thoroughly exasperated, he became implacable and resolute.

"We will recover our men," said Ogier to his son, "and then repay Guillem in his own coin."

"How shall we get the money?" asked Jean.

"You must go to Sarlat, and see if any can be procured there. See the Bishop; he may help."

Accordingly Jean del' Peyra rode back a good part of the way he had traced the previous day, but half-way turned left to Sarlat instead of right to La Roque.

The little city of Sarlat occupies a basin at the juncture of some insignificant streams, and was chosen by the first settlers—monks—as being in an almost inaccessible position, when Périgord was covered with forest. It was to be reached only through difficult and tortuous glens. A flourishing town it never was, and never could be, as it had no fertile country round to feed it. It was a town that struggled on—and drew its main importance from the fact of its serving as a centre of French influence against the all-pervading English power. It had another source of life in that, being under the pastoral staff instead of under the sword, it had better chance of peace than had a town owing duty, military and pecuniary, to a lay lord. The baron, if not on the defensive, was not happy unless levying war, whereas the ecclesiastical chief acted solely in the defensive.

The protection of the district ruled by the Bishop of Sarlat was no easy or inexpensive matter, hemmed in as it was by insolent seigneurs, who pretended to serve the English when wronging their French neighbours. Moreover the strong town of Domme, on the Dordogne, facing La Roque, was in the hands of the English, and was garrisoned for them under the command of the notorious Captain, Le Gros Guillem.

This man had his own fastness above the Vézère, on the left bank, below the juncture of the Beune with the river, a place called by the people "L'Église de Guillem," in bitterness of heart and loathing, because there, according to the popular belief, he had his sanctuary in which he worshipped the devil. Few, if any, of the peasants had been suffered to enter this fortress, half-natural, half-artificial. Such as had gained a closer view than could be obtained from two hundred feet below by the river bank said that it consisted of a series of chambers, partly natural, scooped in the rock, and of a cavern of unknown depth with winding entrance, that led, it was rumoured, into the place of torment; and at the entrance, excavated in a projecting piece of rock, was a holy-water stoup such as is seen in churches. This, however, it was whispered, was filled with blood, and Le Gros Guillem, when he entered the cave to adore the fiend, dipped his finger therein, and signed himself with some cabalistic figure, of which none save he knew the significance.

Between his own stronghold of L'Église and the walled town of Domme, Guillem was often on the move.

Without much difficulty, Jean del' Peyra obtained access to the Bishop, an amiable, frightened, and feeble man, little suited to cope with the difficulties of his situation. Jean told him the reason why he had come.

"But," said the Bishop, "you are not my vassal. I am not bound to sustain you." And he put his hands to his head and pressed it.

"I know that, Monseigneur; but you are French, and so is my father; and we French must hold together and help each other."

"You must go to the French Governor of Guyenne."

"Where is he! What can he do? There is no time to be lost to save the men."

The Bishop squeezed his head. "I am unable to do anything. A hundred livres of Bergerac—that is a large sum. If it had been livres of Tours, it would have been better. Here!"—he signed to his treasurer—"How much have I? Is there anything in my store?"

"Nothing," answered the official. "Monseigneur has had to pay the garrison of La Roque, and all the money is out."

"You hear what he says," said the Bishop dispiritedly. "I have nothing!"

"Then the seven men must be mutilated."

"It is too horrible! And the poor wives and children! Ah! we are in terrible times. I pray the Lord daily to take me out of it into the Rest there remains for the people of God; or, better still, to translate me to another see."

"Yes, Monseigneur; but whilst we are here we must do what we can for our fellows, and to save them from further miseries."

"That is true, boy, very true. I wish I had money. But it comes in in trickles and goes out in floods. I will tell you what to do. Go to the Saint Suaire at Cadouin and pray that the Holy Napkin may help."

"I am afraid the help may come too late! The Napkin, I hear, is slow in answering prayer."

"Not if you threaten it with the Saint Suaire at Cahors. Those two Holy Napkins are so near that they are as jealous of each other as two handsome girls; and if they met would tear each other as cats. Tell the Saint Suaire at Cadouin that if you are not helped at once you will apply to her sister at Cahors."

"I have been told that it costs money to make the Saint Suaire listen to one's addresses, and I want to receive and not to pay."

"Not much, not much!" protested the Bishop.

"Besides, Monseigneur," said the youth, "there might be delay while the two Holy Napkins were fighting out the question which was to help us. And then—to have such a squabble might not be conducive to religion."

"There is something in that," said the Bishop. "Oh, my head! my poor head!" He considered a while, and then with a sigh said—"I'll indulge butter. I will!"

"I do not understand, my lord."

"I'll allow the faithful to eat butter in Lent, if they will pay a few sols for the privilege. That will raise a good sum."

"Yes, but Lent is six months hence, and the men will be mutilated in twelve days."

"Besides, I want the butter money for the cathedral, which is a shabby building! What a world of woe we live in!"

"Monseigneur, can you not help me? Must seven homes be rendered desolate for lack of a hundred livres?"

"Oh, my head! it will burst! I have no money, but I will do all in my power to assist you. Ogier del' Peyra is a good man, and good men are few. Go to Levi in the Market Place. He is the only man in Sarlat who grows rich in the general impoverishment. He must help you. Tell him that I will guarantee the sum. If he will give you the money, then he shall make me pay a denier every time I light my fire and warm my old bones at it. He can see my chimney from his house, and whenever he notices smoke rise from it, let him come in and demand his denier."

"It will take a hundred years like that to clear off the principal and meet the interest."

The Bishop raised his hands and clasped them despairingly. "I have done my utmost!"

"Then I am to carry the tidings to seven wives that the Church cannot help them?"

"No—no! Try Levi with the butter-money. I did desire to have a beautiful tower to my cathedral, but seven poor homes is better than fine carving, and I will promise him the butter-money. Try him with that—if that fails, then I am helpless. My head! my head! It will never rest till laid in the grave. O sacred Napkins of Cadouin and Cahors! Take care of yourselves and be more indulgent to us miserable creatures, or I will publish a mandment recommending the Napkin of Compiègne, or that of Besançon, and then where will you be?"

CHAPTER VI

THE JEW

Jean Del' Peyra left the Bishop's castle, which stood on rising ground above the town, and was well fortified against attack, and entered the city to find Levi. The Jew lived in the little square before the cathedral.

The Bishop might well say that his episcopal seat was shabby, for the minster was small and rude in structure, a building of the Romanesque period such as delighted the monks to erect, and of which many superb examples exist in Guyenne. The monastic body at Sarlat had not been rich enough or sufficiently skilled in building to give themselves as stately a church as Souillac, Moissac, or Cadouin. It consisted, like nearly every other sacred dwelling of the period, of an oblong domed building, consisting of three squares raised on arches surmounted by Oriental cupolas, with an unfinished tower at the west end. The visitor to Sarlat at the present day will see a cathedral erected a century and more after the date of our story, in a debased but not unpicturesque style.

The Jew was not at home. His wife informed Jean that he had gone to La Roque to gather in a few sols that were owing to him there for money advanced to needy personages, and that she did not expect him home till the morrow. Christians were ready enough to come to her husband for loans, but were very reluctant to pay interest, and it cost Levi much pains and vexation to extract what was his due from those whom he had obliged. Accordingly Jean remounted his horse, and rode over the hills due south, in the direction of the Dordogne.

About halfway between Sarlat and La Roque, at the highest point of the road, where the soil is too thin even to sustain a growth of oak coppice, and produces only juniper, Jean passed a singular congeries of stones; it consisted of several blocks set on end, forming an oblong chamber, and covered by an immense slab, in which were numerous cup-like holes, formed by the weather, or whence lumps of flint had been extracted. It was a prehistoric tomb—a dolmen, and went by the name of the Devil's Table. To the present day, the women coming to the market at Sarlat from La Roque rest on it, and if they put their fish which they have to sell into the cups on the table, are sure of selling them at a good price. Yet such action is not thought to bring a blessing with it, and the money got by the sale of the fish thus placed in the Devil's cups rarely does good to those who receive it. The monument is now in almost total ruin: the supports have been removed or are fallen, but at the time of this tale it was intact.

Jean did not pay it any attention, but rode forwards as hastily as he could on his somewhat fatigued horse.

On reaching the little town of La Roque, Jean was constrained to put up his horse outside the gates. There was not a street in the place along which a horse could go. The inhabitants partook of the nature of goats, they scrambled from one house to another when visiting their neighbours. Only by the riverside was there a level space, and this was occupied by strong walls as a protection against assault from the water.

Jean inquired whether the Jew had been seen, and where, and was told that he had been to several houses, and was now in that of the Tardes. The family of Tarde was one of some consequence in the little place, and had its scutcheon over the door. It was noble—about three other families in the place had the same pretensions, or, to be more exact, right. Jean, without scruple, went to the house of the Tardes and asked for admission, and was at once ushered into the little hall.

The Jew was there along with Jean and Jacques Tarde, and they were counting money. To Del' Peyra's surprise, Noémi was also present and looking on.

Jean del' Peyra gave his name, and asked leave to have a word with the Jew. He stated the circumstances openly. There was no need for concealment. Le Gros Guillem had fallen on Ste. Soure, and after committing the usual depredations, had carried off seven men, and held them to ransom. The sum demanded was a hundred Bergerac livres. Unless that sum was produced immediately, the men would be mutilated—hamstrung.

As Jean spoke, with bitterness welling up in his heart, he looked straight in the eyes of Noémi. She winced, changed colour, but resolved not to show that she felt what was said, and returned Jean's look with equal steadiness.

"And you want the money?" said the Jew. "On what security?"

"The Bishop will grant an indulgence to eat butter in Lent at a fee. That will raise more than is required."

"The Bishop!" Levi shook his head. "You Christians are not men of your word. You will promise it—and never pay."

"You lie, Jewish dog!" said Jacques Tarde. "Have I not paid you what was owing?"

"Ah, you—but the Bishop!"

"Is he false?"

"He may think it righteous to cheat the Jew."

"He will give you what security you require that the money be forthcoming," said Jean.

"Will not the Christians eat butter without paying for the dispensation?" asked the Jew. "If they think that the butter-money is coming to me they will not scruple. I do not like the security. The Bishop is old; he may die before Lent; and then what chance shall I have of getting my money? The next Bishop will not allow butter, or, if he does, will pocket the money it brings in. He will not be tied by this Bishop's engagement. I will not have the butter-money."

"Will you take a mortgage on Ste. Soure?" asked Jean.

"I don't know. It is not on the Bishop's lands. It is face to face with the stronghold of the big Guillem. If I wanted to sell and realise, who would buy in such proximity? Whom are you under? The King of France? He is a long way off and his arm is weak. No, I will not have a mortgage on Ste. Soure. Besides, I am poor; I have no money."

"You lying cur!" exclaimed Jacques Tarde; "we have paid you up all the capital lent us. We would no longer have our blood sucked at twenty-eight per cent, and we have sold the little land at Vézac to pay you."

"That was easy land to sell," said the Jew. "With Beynac Castle on one side and La Roque on the other! But Ste. Soure"—he shook his head. "It is under the claw of Guillem. He has but to put down his hand from the Church and he scratches through the roofs, and picks out all that he desires."

"And you refuse the Bishop's guarantee?"

The Jew looked furtively at the two Tardes and at Jean and said—"Who is to guarantee the Bishop? On his lands he sees that I draw in my little sols, but then I pay him for that, I pay heavily, and for that heavy price he allows me to lend moneys and pick up interests. But I do not pay the King of France to ensure me against the Bishop. That is why I will not let him be in debt to me."

"Our land is devoured by two evils," said Jacques Tarde. "The routier and Jew, and I do not know which is worst! We shake ourselves, and kick out, and for a moment are free, and then they settle on us again. The carrion crow and the worm—and so we die."

"Ah, Monsoo Tarde!" answered Levi. "Why do you speak like this? You wished to build you a grand house and paint it and carve and gild—and for that must have moneys. Did I come and force you to borrow of me my poor pennies? Did you not come and beg me to furnish what you needed? I did not say to you, 'Your old house is not worthy of a Tarde. It is mean and not half fine enough for a fine man like you!' It was your own pride and vanity sent you to me. And now, if I could find the moneys would not this young gentleman bless me, and the seven families I might be the saving of, call down the benediction of the skies on me and mine? Here has he come all the way from Ste. Soure to seek me, and he is in despair because I am so poor."

"You poor! Levi! you thief!"

"I am poor. I lay by grain on grain; and such as you scatter and destroy. Why should I spend my painfully gathered pennies to save some of your villains, young Sir? What if there was a riot in Sarlat as there was fifteen years ago—and the mob fell on the Jews? How was it then? Did you not fire our houses, and throw our children into the flames, and run your pikes into the hearts of our mothers and wives? You think we care for you after that! Let your own Christian thieves hamstring their own brothers. Why do you come to poor Levi to help you—to Levi who is helpless among you, and is only suffered to live because he is necessary to you? You cannot do without him, as now—now, amidst the violences of Le Gros Guillem!"

"And you will not help me," said Jean, despairingly. He had no thought for the wrongs endured by the Jews, no thought for what made them a necessity, no thought of the incongruity that while the Church denounced usury, the usurers were only able to carry on their trade by the Pope and the prelates extending their protection to them—for a consideration in hard cash, paid annually.

Again Jean's eyes met those of Noémi; he was pale, his brow clouded, his lips trembled, as though about to address some words to her.

"What would you say?" she asked. "Speak out. I am not afraid to hear. Levi has been making my father responsible for his bloodsucking."

"I would," said Jean sullenly, "I would to Heaven you could come with me and see the work wrought at Ste. Soure; and if after that you were able to laugh and lightly talk of your father as a great man and one to be proud of because he is in every mouth—then, God help you!"

"I will come!" answered the girl impulsively. "When? At once?"

Jean looked at her incredulously.

"Aye!" said she. "Jacques Tarde has nothing to engage him now that he has shaken off the horse-leech. He will ride with me, and we will take another, though I reckon my presence would suffice as a protection. None will lay hands on the daughter of Le Gros Guillem." She reared her head in pride.

"Be not so sure of that," said Jean. "At Ste. Soure they would tear you to pieces if they knew who you were."

"And you—would look on and let it be?"

"No; on my lands, whilst under my protection, you are safe."

"Under your protection!" jeered the girl! "Bah! If I stood among a thousand, and shouted, 'Ware! Le Gros Guillem is on you!' they would fly on all sides as minnows when I throw a stone into the water." She altered her tone and said: "There, I go to do good. I will see my father if he is at his church, and I will whisper good thoughts unto him, and get him to reduce the ransom. Now, will you take me with you?"

"You will trust yourself with me?"

"Jacques Tarde shall come also. Let anyone dare to touch Noémi! I will come. When shall we start?"

"At once," answered Jean.

"So be it; at once."

## CHAPTER VII

THE NEW COMPANION

One of the strangest features of a strange time was the manner in which families were broken up and neighbours were at feud. The same individuals shifted sides and were one day boozing together at table and the next meeting in deadly conflict. Discord was in families. In the house of Limeuil the father was French, the son English; and the son was English merely because he desired to turn his father out of the ancestral heritage and lord it in his room. Limeuil was stormed by the son, then retaken by the father; now sacked by English troops, and then sacked again by French troops, who cared nothing for the national causes of France or England. Prevost de la Force and Perducat d'Albret had castles facing each other on opposite sides of the Dordogne. Each desired to draw some money out of the commercial town of Bergerac on the plea that he was empowered to protect it from the other. Accordingly, one called himself French, the other English; and Perducat, when it suited his convenience, after having been

English, became French. Domestic broils determined the policy of the turbulent seigneurs. If they coveted a bit of land, or a village, or a castle that belonged to a brother or a cousin of one persuasion, they went over to the opposed to supply them with an excuse for falling on their kinsmen. The Seigneur de Pons, because his marriage settlement with his wife did not allow him sufficient liberty to handle her means, turned French, and his wife threw open her gates to the Duke of Lancaster. Whereupon the seigneur fought the English, to whom he had formerly been devoted, retook his town, and chastised his wife. The man who was French to-day was English to-morrow, and French again the day after. Some were very weathercocks, turning with every wind, always with an eye to their own advantage.

Consequently, families were much mixed up with both parties. Unless a seigneur was out on a raid, he would associate on terms of friendliness with the very men whom he would hang on the next occasion. Kinsfolk were in every camp. The seigneurs had allies everywhere; but their kinsfolk were not always their allies—were often their deadliest enemies.

The mother of Noémi was akin to the family of Tarde. Indeed, her aunt was the mother of Jean and Jacques, who were, accordingly, her first cousins. The Tarde family were French; no one in Gageac was English. By interest, by tradition, the place was true to the Lilies.

A little way up the river, on the further side, was Domme, which was held by the English. Noémi passed from the English to the French town, and nothing was thought of it that she was as much at home with her cousins in La Roque Gageac as among her mother's attendants at Domme. Even the young Tardes might have gone to the market in the English town and have returned unmolested.

The bullies of Guillem in like manner swaggered where they listed, penetrated to Gageac, when there was a dance or a drinking bout; and, so long as they came unarmed, were allowed admittance.

No one could say whether there was peace or war. There was a little of one and a little of the other. Whenever a roysterer was weary of doing nothing, he gathered his men together and made a raid; whenever a captain wanted to pay his men, he plundered a village. Otherwise, all went on tolerably quietly. There was no marching across the country of great bodies of armed men, no protracted sieges, no battles in which whole hosts were engaged. But there was incessant fear, there were small violences, there was no certainty of safety. There was no central power to control the wrong-doers, no justice to mete out to them the reward of their deeds. When the lion and the wolf and the bear are hungry, then they raven for food; when glutted, they lie down and sleep. The barons and free captains and little seigneurs were the lions, wolves, and bears that infested Guyenne and Périgord. They were now on the alert and rending, then ensued a period of quietude.

Little passed between Jean del' Peyra and Noémi on the way. She was mounted on a fresh horse, and attended by two serving-men of the Tardes, as Jacques and Jean could not accompany her, having duties connected with the little town to discharge that day which required their presence. Jean del' Peyra was on his fagged steed, and could not keep up with the rest. Jean was not sanguine that the girl would prevail with her father, but he was grateful that she should make the attempt.

On reaching the point at the junction of the Beune with the Vézère where the roads or tracks diverged, the one to the Church of Guillem, the other to the ford at Tayac, Noémi halted till Jean came up.

"I am going to see my father," she said. "I will come on to Ste. Soure when I have his answer—but I trust I shall bring to you your men."

"I thank you," answered the lad.

"Come, Jean," said the girl; "you will not think so ill of me as you have done. Give me your hand."

"I cannot think ill now of one who is doing her best to relieve my father and me in a case of pressing necessity, and of saving seven families from worse than death."

He put out his hand and pressed hers, but without cordiality. The hand he took was that of the daughter of the scourge of the country. He could not forget that; he touched the hand of the child of the man who had brought desolation into the home of the Rossignols.

Noémi left the attendants with her horse at the foot of the steep ascent that led to the Church of Guillem.

The ascent was up a slope of crumbled chalk and flints hardly held together by a little wiry grass, some straggling pinks, and bushes of box and juniper. The incline was as rapid as that of a Gothic house-roof. Of path there was none, for every man who scrambled up mounted his own way, and his footprints sent shale and dust over the footprints of his predecessor. The plateau through which the river has sawn its way is some four hundred feet at the highest point above the bed of the stream; in some places the cliffs are not only perpendicular, they overhang. They rise at once from the river that washes their bases and undermines them, or from the alluvial flats that have been formed by floods. This was not the case at L'Église Guillem. The stronghold of Guillem occupied a terrace in the abrupt scarp where it rose out of an immense slope of rubble, very much as at Ste. Soure, a little below it on the further bank. Here, as there, the rubble slope was a protection as great as a precipice. It was not as difficult to climb, but it could not be climbed without those in the stronghold being able to roll down rocks, discharge weapons at such as were laboriously endeavouring to mount. Noémi reached a spring that issued from the side of the cliff in a dribble, was received in a basin, and the overflow nourished a dense growth of maidenhair-fern and moss. It was thence that the occupants of the castle derived their drinking-water. Hard by was the gateway. Here she was challenged, gave her name, and was admitted.

L'Église Guillem was oddly constructed. The depth of the caves or concave shelters was not great, not above twelve to fifteen feet, consequently would not admit of chambers and halls in which many men could move about. To gain space, beams had been driven into the natural wall of rock at the back of the caves, and brought forward to project some eight feet over the edge of the cliff. On these projecting rafters walls of timber filled in with stone had been erected, and lean-to roofs added to cover them, socketed into the cliff above the opening mouth of the cave or series of caves. This is still a method of construction in the country, with this exception—that such modern dwellings are not pendulous in mid-air, as were those of the free captains, but are now on solid floors, and consist of rooms, one half of which are caves, and the other half artificial excrescences.

By means of this overhanging portion of the castle, by a ladder a chamber could be reached, cut out in the face of the cliff immediately above the mouth of the natural cavern, a chamber at the present day visible, but absolutely inaccessible, since the wooden excrescence has disappeared by which it was reached. This upper chamber was the treasury of the castle.

To the present day not two miles up the valley of the Beune is a hamlet, a cluster of houses, called Grioteaux, built in a huge cave, but with the fronts somewhat beyond the upper lip of the cave; and in the face of the precipice above is precisely such a treasure-chamber, only to be reached by means of a ladder from the roof of the house below it.

"What—you here!" exclaimed the Great Guillem in surprise, when he saw the girl enter the one room in which were himself and his men, about a table, on which were scattered chalices from churches, women's jewellery, silken dresses, even sabots plucked off the feet of peasants. The captain was dividing spoil.

The Great Guillem was much as Jean del' Peyra had described him—tall, gaunt, with a high head, and baldness from his forehead to the crown, his hair sandy and turning grey, dense bushy red eyebrows, the palest of blue eyes, and a profusion of red hair about his jaws. The mouth was large, with thin lips, and teeth wide apart and pointed, as though they had been filed sharp. Men said he had a double row in his jaw. It was the mouth of a shark.

"Come here, little cat!" shouted the freebooter. "Here are we dogs of war dividing the plunder."

"What plunder, father? Did you get all these silks and trinkets from Ste. Soure?"

"From Ste. Soure indeed! Not that; nothing thence but wine-casks and grain; and a fine matter we have had hauling the barrels up into our kennel. What do you want with us, child?"

The girl looked at the men; there were a dozen, and her father the thirteenth. They were in rough and coarse clothing, each with a red cross on his left arm—a badge of allegiance to the Cross of St. George. Some of the companies wore a white or blue cross when serving no political party, but the Great Guillem was ostensibly in the English service, and as such had been given the commandantship of Domme. The men had been drinking, and were flushed, partly with wine, partly with excitement, as the division of the plunder was made by lot, the lot being a knucklebone in a bassinet. A lawless, insolent company, and one difficult to treat with.

Noémi was puzzled what to do. But she was a bold, spirited girl, and she said: "This is the first time I have been here. I claim largesse."

"Largesse!" laughed one of the men; "I say—the first time anyone enters he pays footing."

"He, yes," said the girl; "but with a woman it is other. I claim largesse."

"What do you mean? A share of the loot?"

"A large share," answered Noémi.

"I have two lots to one; I will surrender one to you," said Guillem.

"Of all the spoil?"

"Of all for which we are raffling."

"And the men—the seven men you took?"

"They are not in the game. We wait till the ransom comes, and that will be divided not by lot but by shares. Money is so divided, not—" Her father tossed over some odds and ends with which the table was cumbered.

"I want the seven men," said Noémi.

A roar of laughter greeted this demand.

"A hundred livres! That is a fine largesse," said one.

"It cannot be," said Guillem. "They belong to us all."

"Little one," shouted one half-drunken fellow, "we only divide among ourselves—merry companions. We take from those who are outside the band."

"But I am the Captain's daughter."

"That matters not; you are not a companion."

"Father, give me a lot."

"I will—my lot."

"And grant me a request."

"If you draw the highest lot, you shall have what you will—save a share in the loot, and to that you can have no right. We have our laws and are bound to abide by them."

"Let us draw, then."

The bassinet was passed round, and each drew. There were fourteen knucklebones in it. Noémi put in her hand first and drew, then each in succession.

"Hands open," shouted Guillem, and each fist was thrust forward on the table and opened flat, exposing the bone. The knuckles were numbered up to fourteen.

"Fourteen!" exclaimed Guillem, as he looked at the rude die in his daughter's palm.

"Best of three," said a man.

"Again!" called the Captain, after the bones had been thrown into the bassinet and shaken.

The same proceeding was gone through. Again each hand was exposed on the table.

"Fourteen again!"

"A woman and the devil have luck!" shouted one of the men. "There is no beating that!"

"Aye! but there is. If next time she draws one," retorted another. "She is a woman; I wish her well."

"Ah! you Roger; always honour the petticoat."

"Again!" thundered the Captain.

Once more hands were plunged into the iron cap, withdrawn, and placed clenched on the table.

"Reveal!" cried Guillem, and immediately the hands were turned up with the knuckle-bones.

"Fourteen!" again he shouted, as he held up the piece his daughter had exposed.

"Was ever luck like this!" stormed one man. "And I—I never draw above five."

"Well; what is your request?" asked Guillem.

"You have sworn to grant it me."

"Yes; if not against rule."

"Then make me one of the Company!"

A pause, then a shout: "The Red Cross! The Red Cross! Vive the new Companion!"

In an instant a piece of crimson silk brocade, an ecclesiastical vestment, was torn to shreds, and the rough hands of the freebooters were fastening two strips crosswise to Noémi's arm.


CHAPTER VIII

IN THE DEVIL'S CUPS

"A new companion must justify his election," said the sullen man, who had throughout shown ill disposition towards Noémi.

"The new companion shall do so," answered Noémi. A deep colour flushed her olive skin. "For that I ask you to follow me, as well as that other comrade who was as inclined to be civil as you to be insolent. First, send down below and bid the two servants of the Tardes go on to Ste. Soure and tarry there till I go for them."

"You—to Ste. Soure?" said her father.

"Not now. But I do not desire to have the Tardes' men with me. They are not of the Company."

"What do you mean?"

"That I will justify my election," said Noémi. "And for that I take these two mates—and no others."

"It is not well that I go," said the sulky man. "But, if go I must, it is unwillingly."

"And I go with all my heart," said he whose name was Roger.

"What do you intend to do, child?" asked her father, puzzled and uneasy. "This is a farce. Take off the cross."

"No, it is no farce. I will not remove the cross till I have shown that I am worthy to be enrolled in your band."

"Then what will you do?"

"That is my secret."

"And you demand two of the companions?"

"Yes; two of the companions—he named Roger, and—"

"Amanieu?"

"Roger and Amanieu. I ask that they may accompany me and serve me and do my bidding—on my first chevauchée."

"La Pucelle! Another Joan! To the English! To the English! Vive la Pucelle de Domme! We will pit her against the Pucelle de Domrémi." The men shouted, hammered the table, and tossed the knucklebones about. They treated the matter as a joke.

Amanieu, the sulky man, was very angry at being fixed upon to make one of a party that would incur ridicule and expose him to the jeers of his fellows.

Le Gros Guillem now interfered. "If my daughter has said you are to attend, and I consent, you go. Guard her well."

Amanieu murmured no more. There was no insubordination in a Company.

The serving-men of the Tarde brothers were dismissed, and then Noémi prepared to depart along with her new attendants. Her father asked no further questions. The horses were brought from a stable cut in the rocks. They were nimble and sure of footing. Access to the stable was only to be had by a drawbridge let fall over a chasm, and from the further side of the gap a narrow track descended rapidly to the bottom of the valley.

At Noémi's request the men had drawn on jackets that concealed their red crosses, and no one seeing the little party would have conjectured that the girl was attended by some of the greatest ruffians and cut-throats in the country. She knew the character of the men, but was not afraid. The fear of her father entertained by all the band, and the discipline maintained in the Company, would prevent them from doing her harm.

Guillem was a man of few words, but of decision in action. The look of his pale eyes was enough, as he sent the men with Noémi, to take from them any spirit of insolence or rebellion had they entertained it. They knew without more words than the three uttered by Guillem, that if she came to harm through them, by their neglect, in any way, he was the man to put them to death by slow and horrible torture. They had seen that done once on a comrade who had disregarded a half-expressed order. He had been roasted over a slow fire.

The two men asked no questions when Noémi took the road to Sarlat, and along the road she did not speak with them. At Sarlat she bade them hold back while she went on alone and on foot to make an inquiry. Apparently satisfied at what she had learnt, she returned to the men, remounted her horse, and said, "Forward!"

She rode along the way to La Roque, a little ahead of the two men. The day was closing in. It would be dark by the time they reached her home.

Presently they came to a long and tedious ascent. The way had been at one time paved, but had not been repaired for a century. It ran up a hog's back or hill, through coppice that was cut every fourteen years for the making of charcoal, direct to the point where was the Devil's Table.

She halted, and turned to her followers; and they drew rein.

"Listen to me," she said. "You do not know whither I am leading you, for what purpose you follow me, or what is to be gained thereby. But one thing you do know, that you are placed under my command by Le Gros Guillem, and that you disobey at your peril. I will tell you wherefore you are following me; it is for your own advantage. You have carried away seven men from the Del' Peyras, and you have put them to ransom at a hundred livres. That is a large sum. It is to be divided among you into fourteen equal shares. But let me tell you that if this sum be not found—you will get nothing. The seven men will be no gain to you when cast away mutilated. Jean del' Peyra has been this day to Sarlat, he has been to the Bishop, he has been to the Jew Levi, he has been to the Tardes at Gageac, I cannot say where he has not been, to whom he has not applied—but nowhere can he raise the sum. It was too large. But that is no concern of mine. The money must be found, or you get nothing. I can tell you where the sum is to be found, whence it can be taken. But understand this—no more shall be exacted than the hundred livres. I will not have a denier more, nor a denier less. You agree to this?"

"Yes, we shall be glad of the money; we do not want to hurt the men of Ste. Soure, and their wounds are no pay to us."

"Very well. Then we understand each other. You would never receive any ransom but for me. It is I who bring you where it shall be paid."

"And where is that?" asked Amanieu.

"On the Devil's Table," answered Noémi.

The men shrank back. Their superstitious fears were aroused.

"Do not be alarmed. We shall not conjure up the foul fiend; but we shall squeeze one of his servants. Let us ride on and await him at the Table."

Then she turned towards La Roque, and in silence they continued to ascend the hill.

When they had nearly reached the summit she drew up again, and said to the men—

"I will explain it all. The Jew Levi comes this way. He has been gathering in money at La Roque, and my cousins have paid him a large sum. He has been engaged there all day, and he made my cousins, the Tardes, promise to send servants with him to see him safe on his way back to Sarlat. They agreed to send him on his way as far as the Devil's Table; and he named the time at which he would be ready to start. I know, if he has started on his way as he proposed, that he will be approaching now. From the Table onward to Sarlat he would be alone, but alone he could not convey all the money. What he purposes doing I cannot say. We will wait and see. He desired that he might be attended all the way to Sarlat, but that the Tardes would not allow. The distance was too great, the men were needed, they would not be home till too late. He was forced to accept half of what he had asked. Understand, no more is to be taken from the Jew than the ransom money. It were better that a Jew should lose than that seven Christian households should be ruined."

The men laughed. They were easy in their minds now that they understood they were to play a familiar game—only they grudged that they were to half accomplish it. If they caught a Jew let them squeeze and wring him out till not a drop of the golden syrup were left in him.

Noémi had, however, her own ideas in the matter. She justified her act to her conscience as a deed of necessity. It was a marvel that her conscience felt any scruple in the matter, as in the Middle Ages none hesitated to defraud a Jew, none considered that a son of Israel had any right to have meted out to him the like justice as to a Christian. Before the Cathedral gates at Toulouse every Good Friday a Jew had to present himself to have his ears boxed by the Bishop, and to acknowledge in his person on behalf of his race its guilt in having crucified the Messiah.

"Here!" said the girl, "tie up your horses and mine and lie in the scrub."

Before them, on the left hand of the track, rose the Devil's Table; a mound of earth had anciently covered it, but rain had washed away the earth from the capstone and showed the points of those blocks which upheld it. The slab was a singularly uncouth stone, with its flat old bed underneath, the upper surface uneven and dinted with cup-holes.

The routiers had not been long in hiding before the voice of Levi was heard, and the tramp of his ass.

"I thank you, good fellows. It was gracious of your master to lend me your escort, for, Heaven knows! I am too poor to need one. My ass is laden with lentils. You eat them in your fasting times, and when not fasting, eat pig. I cannot touch the unclean meat, and so eat lentils all the year. All my little moneys I carried with me have been expended in lentils for my wife Rachel and me. Ah! this must last us a long time. We are so poor, and lentils are so dear."

"You will give us something to drink your health, Levi," asked one of Tardes' men.

"Oh! certainly. Open both your hands and I will fill them with lentils. When Daniel, Shadrach, Meshach, and Abednego were in the palace of King Darius, they refused the meats from the King's table that they might eat lentils. And they grew fat! Oh! Father Abraham, so sleek that their faces shone, and all the young ladies ran after them. Open your hands and I will give you lentils, and all the fair maids of La Roque will admire you."

The men laughed. "Come, come, Jew, keep the pulse for yourself, and give us something more solid—money—and we will drink your health."

"Money!" exclaimed Levi; "as if I had money! Oh, Fathers of the Covenant! poor Levi with money!—that is a comica idea. You are jesting with me, and I like a jest."

Those lying in wait listened to the altercation that ensued—the men murmured, then there ensued an outcry from the Jew and a burst of laughter from the men—they had raised and thrown down on the ground the sack which the ass was carrying.

The Jew shouted and entreated and swore, but to no avail. The two serving-men ran off on their way back to La Roque Gageac, full of glee, rejoicing that they had served the man such a trick, for they well knew that he would hardly be able to replace the sack on his ass.

After Levi had convinced himself that his appeals were in vain, he returned to the fallen sack, and vainly endeavoured to lift it upon the ass. He could raise it at one end, but not bear the entire weight. He became very angry, and grumbled and cursed, and prayed to Heaven for assistance.

Then, as his sole chance, he endeavoured to roll the sack up the sepulchral mound, and so to tilt it on to the Devil's Table. By that means, if he drew up his ass by the mouth of the burial-chamber, where treasure-seekers had grubbed and made a hollow, he hoped to be able to replace the burden on the back that was to bear it.

"Oh, Fathers Abraham, Isaac, and Mother Sarah!" lamented the Jew, "come to me in my necessity and help me."

"We are here!"

Hands were laid on his shoulder. With a scream of fear he sprang back, and saw two male and a female figure before him. Dusk had set in, and he could not distinguish who they were.

"Jew!" said Noémi, "we want a hundred livres."

"A hundred lentils! Let me go! Help me with my sack, and they are yours."

"Jew!" said the girl; "do not delay us and yourself. We will escort you within sight of the lights of the town—when you have paid us the hundred livres."

"Hear her, Father Abraham!" cried the unhappy man. "She thinks that I have money, who have only a few lentils on which to feed my wife and me."

"I know what you have," said Noémi. "You have all the money paid you by the Tardes."

"It is a lie—I have been paid no money; I have been given a sack of lentils instead."

"Levi—I was present when it was paid."

"You—you are a Tarde! and the Tardes are thieves!"

"I am not a Tarde."

"You are a Tarde—and these are Tardes' servants, and you will cheat and rob me. I shall appeal to the Bishop!"

"Strike a light," said the girl. "Let the man see who we are."

With a flint and steel Amanieu produced sparks, and presently held a wisp of dry grass blazing over his head.

"Look here," said Noémi. "Do you know this?" She showed the red cross on her arm. "Look at the shoulders of my mates. Do you know who they are? Do you know me? I am Le Gros Guillem's daughter. Open your sack."

"Oh, pity me! Pity me!" sobbed the terrified Jew.

"One hundred livres—not a denier under, not a denier over," answered the girl. "See, in the Devil's Table are ten saucers; put ten livres into each, and you, Amanieu, and you, Roger, count. Jew, when the last coin is paid, you shall go on with the rest. You do not stir till the sum is paid that I require."

The Jew faltered, trembled, stuttered some unintelligible words.

"Levi!" said Noémi, "you know how Guillem's men deal with the refractory. Ho! a string here for his thumbs."

The ten cups were filled.

CHAPTER IX

A SINGED GLOVE

A commotion, suppressed in outward manifestation, agitated Ste. Soure. Very little work was being done in the fields and vineyards. What work was done had little reference to agriculture.

Men hurried about, but were cautious not to allow it to be seen by anyone at a distance what their occupation was.

In a place like Ste. Soure, in a valley between precipices, nothing was easier than for a spy to observe all that was going on in a village. If on this occasion one commissioned by the Captain of the Free Company that occupied l'Église Guillem had stationed himself at a suitable point, he would have seen that Ste. Soure was alive, but would not have been able to distinguish what engaged the inhabitants.

He would, indeed, have noticed the peasants bringing together their faggots of vine-prunings, have heard the bleating of sheep that were being killed, and later, had the wind blown his way, have noticed that the air was impregnated with the odour of melted tallow.

That the people of Ste. Soure should be in a condition of more liveliness than usual would not have surprised him, after the event of the rush made on the place by the Free Companions, and the capture of some of the householders.

But no spy was sent to observe the doings of the villagers. The usual watch was kept from the eyrie of the Church of Guillem, but from it the village of Ste. Soure and the Castle of Le Peuch were not visible.

The sudden raid had so quelled the inhabitants that no danger was anticipated from that quarter. What was Ogier del' Peyra but a little Seigneur? So little that it was not worth while for any of the big men in the neighbourhood to sustain his cause. In those rough times the small men were pinched out. Only the great ones held their own. There was no security for any man who stood in independence, unless he were very great indeed. In an earlier age the soil had belonged to many hundreds and thousands of free landholders, who owed no man anything except a slight tax in money or kind to the Duke of Aquitaine or to the Count of Périgord. But that condition of affairs was past. The little freemen had been broken in pieces by the violence of the marauders, of the barons, by their own mutual quarrels, and nearly all had surrendered their independence into the hands of great Seigneurs in their neighbourhood; they had given up their freedom in return for assurance of protection.

Ogier del' Peyra, however, represented one of the few families which had not thus passed into vassalage. For that very reason he was viewed askance by the barons of the neighbourhood, to whichever faction they belonged; and as none of them were bound to sustain his cause, not one of them, as Ogier well knew, would draw sword in his behalf against so redoubtable an adversary as Le Gros Guillem, and would be still less inclined to advance him money.

Not only did Ogier know this, but the Free Captain knew it also; and, knowing it, thought it not worth the pains to observe the movements of the man he had plundered, and whom he despised.

One thing did Guillem regret—that he had not taken Le Peuch, the refuge and stronghold of the Del' Peyras; but just as Ogier knew his weakness and insulation, so had he accumulated precautions against attack. His fortress, or castle, was situated in a similar position to that of Guillem, at the head of a steep rubble slope, but it was stronger immeasurably than that of the "Church," for the cliff above it was vastly more lofty, and it was literally honeycombed with chambers. It was precisely due to the fact that the habitation of the family was in the rock, and of the rock, as already intimated, that they had received their name of Del' Peyra. Had not the villagers been completely taken by surprise when the Companions fell on Ste. Soure, they would have carried off their valuables, and taken refuge themselves in inaccessible places, and left only their empty houses to be ransacked by the freebooters.

Long exemption from molestation had made them careless.

It was customary with the robber bands not to devastate the hamlets and villages and farms in their immediate neighbourhood. They needed the daily supplies of food that the peasants could furnish, and they bought these, and maintained a good understanding with the peasantry. When they foraged it was at a distance. It was precisely because "l'Église" was so near to Ste. Soure that the villagers had not anticipated an onslaught.

Now, although the peasants on the opposite side of the river, who were under the shadow of the crags occupied by the routiers knew themselves to be safe, and found a market for their produce, yet they had no love for their tyrannisers. They were sufficiently shrewd to be aware that they were exposed to be plundered, their houses wasted, their wives and daughters carried off by other freebooters, or even by ordinary Companions-in-Arms, such as claimed to serve the French. The Counts of Périgord—who should have been their protectors—were leaders in violence, at the head of several lawless bands, and usually marched under the leopards, so that the ban of the French king had been launched against one Count after another, and he only returned to allegiance for a moment, to break faith at the first occasion. The Castle of Montignac, the headquarters of these countly scoundrels, lay high up the same valley of the Vézère; and the ruffians of the Count passed up and down it, traversing the fields and villages continually. It was to them a matter of supreme indifference which crown was supposed to exercise authority and afford protection where they went, for neither possessed any real authority, neither afforded the smallest protection.

Ogier del' Peyra sat in the porch of the church issuing orders, and his son was by him.

All at once a child on the roof of the church cried out—

"I see—I see—seven men coming, and a lady riding; and I think one is our Petiton."

"What! our men!" exclaimed Ogier; and Jean ran to the roof of the church to look.

He was down directly after. "Father, there is no doubt of it. Gros Guillem's daughter is bringing them here."

"As a gift? Does he restore them free of ransom?" exclaimed Ogier. "If so we cannot proceed."

"I will run and meet them," said Jean.

The tidings spread like wildfire that the men who had been carried off were on their way home. Jean hastened to the river side and was ferried over.

"I have brought them!" said Noémi when she saw him. Her eye was flashing with pleasure. "See—they are all here."

"Did your father surrender them?"

She laughed. "I bought them. I paid the ransom."

"You! Where did you get the money?"

"See." She exposed her arm with the red cross. "I won my spurs. I robbed the Jew. Now you do not think so ill of me, say that." She leaned from her horse to look into his eyes.

He averted his face.

"I thank you for the men. I hate the deed."

"The man was but a Jew!" pleaded Noémi.

"And a robbery is but a robbery," answered Jean.

The girl bit her lips and frowned.

"This is what I get by that I have done, and I have ridden all night to gratify you. I asked my father. I entreated that the men might be let go free. He would not hearken. Then I did this. I could not get the men discharged in any other way. Let them go back," said the girl sullenly; "back into bonds and be served as was threatened. You are content so long as the Jew has his moneys."

"Not so. The men are free—they cannot go back. I had rather they had been freed by any other means."

"And by any other person—say it all!"

"I will not say that. There, Noémi," said the young man, laying his hand on the horse's neck, "I know you meant kindly and right by us. It is not your fault; it is the fault of your blood; it is the fault of the times that you have gone about it in a wrong way."

"There was no other way."

"I do not say that. I was going to Bergerac to raise the money there."

"And pawn your inheritance to a Christian usurer who is worse than a Jew. You have your men, you have your land—be content. If wrong is done, I did it." Noémi abandoned her horse and entered the ferry-boat with the men and Jean.

The joy, the tears, the passionate affection with which the recovered men were welcomed, clung to by their wives and children and friends, moved the girl, and her cheek grew pale and her eyes filled. Jean observed the emotion and said nothing to her, but to himself he breathed: "She is not heartless! The good is not all dead in her."

Some of the women, supposing rightly that the men owed their release to Noémi, but not knowing who she was, came to her, took her hand, kissed it, knelt and put to their lips the hem of her skirt. She was abashed, and shrank back.

"You shall see," said Jean. "I will show you from what you have saved these poor fellows!"

He led her into the cottage of the Rossignols, and she remained silent, apparently cold, looking at the crippled man.

"Can you sit up?" she asked, after a long pause.

"Sit up—yes," he said, and moved his elbow and heaved himself up; "but it opens the wounds again."

"And—can you put your feet down?"

"Feet; I'll never do that more."

"Nor stand?"

"God help me! Never stand before man, never kneel before God. I'm a young man; I'm five-and-twenty, and have got three children. I'll never do aught but lie as a log all the years I have to live!"

"There is a trifle for you," said Noémi, putting money into his hand. "I would I had more. Hush! I cannot bear that!"

The poor woman, still half distraught, now worked to further excitement by the return of the seven men safe and sound, while her own husband lay in irrecoverable wretchedness, broke into a storm of curses against Le Gros Guillem, and of blasphemy against God. It was more horrible to hear her than to see the man, who bore his lot not so much with patience as with stolidity.

Then in came Ogier del' Peyra.

"So," said he, "you have released my men! Did Le Gros Guillem let them pass out of his hands for nothing?"

"I paid him the hundred livres," said Noémi, speaking with difficulty. Something was in her throat choking her.

"Then," said Ogier, "we owe him no debt?"

"None at all."

"And you are returning there—I mean to him—to the Church?"

"I go to see him again."

"What debt of gratitude we owe is to you—not to him?"

Noémi nodded.

"Then, let me say this: Do not stay at the Church."

"I am not going to stay there. I shall but say farewell to—" the girl hesitated, looked at the crippled Rossignol, at his crazy wife, and concluded her sentence in an undertone—"to him, and then away to Domme."

"It is well. Mark my words. Do not stay there—not a night—not a night."

"Why so?"

"Why so? Do you ask that? Is not the wrath of God hanging as a thundercloud over that rock? Is it not full charged with lightnings? When it bursts will it spare the innocent? Will it not involve all in one sudden destruction? Mark my words: do not tarry there—no, not an hour. Your men who came with you are here. They are at Le Peuch, and ready to attend you on your return. Do not tarry. Take counsel. L'Église de Guillem is no place for innocent maidens. It is no church where are holy thoughts and devout prayers—it is the Church of the Foul Fiend, and the mouth of the bottomless pit yawns there."

"I thank you," said Noémi. "I know what it is. I am not going to tarry there."

"There is one favour I ask of you," said the old man. "It is to take a message from me to—to the Big Guillem."

"I will take it."

"Tell him that when one gentleman is about to do the other the favour of a visit he sends a notice that he is coming. That is true courtesy. He forgot to do that to me. I was not ready to receive him with hospitality. Now, render me the grace to hand him this."

Ogier extended to the girl a leather glove singed by fire and the ends of the fingers burnt off.

Noémi hesitated to take it.

"Do not fear," said the old man; "it will not hurt you. It is but a token. Your fa—I mean Le Gros Guillem, will accept the courtesy. Take it, and go."

An hour later Noémi was in the Church of Guillem and before her father.

Somewhat hesitatingly she held out to him the singed glove.

"The Sieur del' Peyra sends you this," she said.

Le Gros Guillem took the glove, threw it on the table, and burst out laughing.

"The mouse defies the lion! Good! This is good! I thank you, Noémi, for bringing me this; it is a right merry jest. I drink to his visit! May he come speedily."

CHAPTER X

BY FIRE

A strange stillness came over the Vézère valley that evening at sundown. Hardly a man was about, not a sound was heard save the barking of a dog in a farm on one side of the river, and the answer of another dog in one on the further side. There was, however, a mysterious hiss in the air about every dwelling and cluster of habitations. Now and then a woman was seen, but it was to call in her children who had run out, and, forgetful of all that had passed, had begun to play.

The sun went down in the west, painting the rocks on the left bank of the Vézère a daffodil yellow, and then slowly a cold, death-like grey stole over the landscape. With the sun the life had gone; and yet, strange to say, no sooner had this dead glaze come over the face of Nature than the human beings woke to activity and began to issue from their houses, cautiously at first, then with greater boldness as the shadows thickened. The men bore their reaping-hooks, their pruning-knives strapped to the end of poles, converting them into formidable weapons. Others had their bills thrust through their leather belts; and every bill and knife was fresh sharpened, explaining the significance of the strange hiss which had been in the air. It had been caused by the grindstones and the files in every house.

Presently the men who had been standing in knots were marshalled into two distinct parties or bands. One, armed with their extemporised halberds and lances, remained in Ste. Soure under Ogier, whereas the other division, laden with sacks, with casks, with loads of faggots, passed over the river, were joined by a contingent from the left bank of the Vézère, and proceeded to ascend the hills. Behind this party, borne by four men, was Rossignol, lying on his bed. His wife desired to follow, and was with difficulty restrained and sent back to take care of her children. Silently, patiently, the men ascended the steep flanks of the hillside, each bearing his burden; even the wounded Rossignol endured the inevitable jerking without a murmur.

A word must here be given to explain the salient character of the country. Originally a vast region in Périgord—the Black Périgord, as it was called from its sombre woods and deep cleft ravines, was one plateau of hard chalk, raised from six hundred and fifty to nine hundred feet above the sea. At some geologic period difficult to define an immense rush of water passed over the plain and tore every rent formed by the upheaval of the chalk into gorge and gully, down which the furious waters poured, scooping out the sides and tearing themselves away. The course taken by the flood is easily recognisable by this fact—that it has left its wash on the tops of the plateau, where to the present day lies a film of caoline, that is to say of feldspathic clay, the produce of the granite ranges to the north and north-east; and this caoline lies in some places in considerable pockets, white as chalk, and only distinguishable from chalk by the experienced eye, and lies in sufficiently important beds to be worked and exported to porcelain factories. Nay, more than this: on the top of these great plateaux of chalk are strewn boulders and pebbles of volcanic production, that were derived unmistakably from the far away Auvergne mountains.

The flood that swirled over the chalk plains not only tore them into islets, and ate out paths through every chink, but also left the surfaces undulating, having washed away what beds were soft and left those which were hard.

These plateaux are more or less untenanted by human beings, because more or less soilless. They are given over to forest or to baldness.

The ravines, the river-valleys, are walled in by precipices with gulfs here and there in their sides where the rock has crumbled away, or caverns have collapsed, and which allow, as lateral combes, access to the riverside. Up such a combe did the peasants now toil, zigzagging, corkscrewing their way, far to the rear of the headland of l'Église Guillem, and wholly invisible from it.

The Captain had so far paid attention to the challenge conveyed by the scorched glove as to give the sentinel on the gate-tower warning to be on the alert, but he had neglected to post anyone on the top of the cliff that overhung his eagle nest. He anticipated no danger from that quarter, for his castle was inaccessible thence, unless, what was inconceivable, assailants should descend on him like spiders from above, at the end of ropes.

"Bah!" scoffed the Chieftain; "a boor! What is Del' Peyra but a country clown? I will teach him such a lesson in a day or two as will make him skip. There is not a Seigneur in the land will lend him half-a-dozen horsemen."

There was, however, an incident in the past that had entirely escaped the memory of Guillem, even if he had heard of it.

At the end of the twelfth century, a carpenter, Durand by name, had roused the peasants to free themselves of their oppressors. What the king could not, what the nobles would not do, that they had done. They had assembled in great multitudes, assumed a white linen hood, called themselves "The Brotherhood of Peace," and hoped to initiate an era of tranquillity by massacring without mercy every routier in the land. They had butchered many thousands, had defeated them in pitched battles, but had themselves been quelled by a combination of the nobles when they attempted to interfere with their turbulence.

That was a matter of two centuries ago, and was not likely to be repeated. Two hundred years of the scourge had whipped every vestige of independence out of the peasants. The Free Companion of the fourteenth and fifteenth century no more feared a combination against him among the peasants than the latter anticipated a revolt in his henroost whence he gathered his eggs. But something had occurred in the north of the land—in France proper—the rumour of which had travelled throughout the country, and which, dimly, feebly, had brought out the idea of national feeling in the south—that was the great success of the French under the Maid of Orleans. Heaven had interfered; the Saints had interested themselves for the afflicted people, for the humbled Crown. The Spirit of God, as in the days of old, had raised up a deliverer—and that deliverer a woman.

The advent of the Maid of Domrémi was of the past, but not forgotten. There was something in the story of Joan to rouse the imagination of a lively and excitable people, and to make them believe that the time was come when Heaven would interfere to assist their feeble arms.

The outrage committed at Ste. Soure on Rossignol, the threat hanging over seven others, had served to rouse the peasantry of the neighbourhood, and as one man they placed themselves under the direction of Ogier, a Seigneur indeed, but in so small a way, as to be but a step removed from the peasant; a man whom they could almost consider as one of themselves, and yet sufficiently raised above them to be able to command obedience, and not incur their jealousy.

As the train of laden men toiled up the ascent, they were joined by charcoal-burners from the coppice with their forks, who fell in, relieved some of the most heavily burdened and said no word. One resolution, one hate, animated the whole mass, combined to make one effort to shake off the detested incubus. It was marvellous how rapidly and how quietly the conjuration had been formed.

When the body of men had reached the top of the hill and were on the plain, they found men there awaiting them from villages beyond, animated by the same spirit, ready to move in the same direction, and to carry out the warfare in the same way, for they also were laden like those from Ste. Soure.

The whole troop now advanced through the brushwood to the bare space above the precipice where trees were scanty.

The night had become very obscure. It was hard to distinguish where the foot could be placed in safety. The very dearth of trees, moreover, warned the men to advance with extreme caution.

Jean del' Peyra had drawn a white sleeve over his right arm, and this was visible in the murkiness of ever-deepening darkness. With this white arm he gave the signals. Orders were communicated in whispers. Behind, under the coppice, at no great distance, was a charcoal-burner's heap. The men who attended to the steaming pile stood by it with their spades and prongs.

Jean raised his white arm. At once those behind him in a chain did the same. At the signal a charcoal-burner drove his fork into the fuming mass, made an opening, and a flame shot up. Next moment a sod was cast on the gap and the flame extinguished.

One, two, three, four—to twenty-five, counted Jean. Again he lifted his white arm. Again the signal was telegraphed back to the charcoal-burners, and again was an opening made and a tongue of fire shot up, to be again instantly extinguished.

One, two, three, four—to twenty-five. A third time Jean raised his arm, and a third time the gleam of flame mounted and was blotted out.

A pause of expectation.

Then from the valley—from the further side of the Vézère—a flash.

One, two, three, four—to twenty-five.

A second flare.

One, two, three, four—to twenty-five.

A third gleam.

"My father is ready," whispered Jean. "Now we must find the exact spot."

It is one thing to know where is a cave or, indeed, any object marking the face of a cliff when seen from below and quite another to discover that same cave, to find out when and where you are immediately above it as you walk on the summit of the precipice. Every feature that marks a site as seen from below fails when you stand above.

If this be the case in broad daylight what must it be by night?

There was but one way in which Jean del' Peyra could discover the exact position of the Church of Guillem, and that was by being held by the feet and extending himself, lying prostrate, over the edge of the cliff. Leaning over the abyss he looked below and to the right and left in the darkness, then signed to be withdrawn.

"Too much to the left!" he said.

He walked cautiously along the edge till he came to what he believed to be the right spot. Again he was extended over the brink, and was again out in his reckoning.

A third attempt was more successful. With a rapid wave of his hand he signed, and was drawn back.

"I have looked down their chimney," he said, "and heard their laughter come up with the reek, and seen the glow of their hearth. Here! build it here!"

At once a hundred hands were engaged in piling up faggots, heaping casks on them and emptying the sacks over the wood. These sacks had been filled with mutton fat. Stones also were planted on the extreme edge. The process was slow. Caution had to be used lest any of the combustible matter should fall over before set alight, and, dropping on the projecting roof or galleries, give the alarm.

The wall of stones erected outside the faggots served a double purpose. In the first place it contained the masses of pine-wood and other combustibles, and preserved them from lapse, but the main object aimed at was, when overthrown, to break in the tiles of the roof so as to allow the molten pitch from the barrels and the flaming tallow to run in among the woodwork and set it on fire. But for this, there would be no assurance of success.

Considerable time was allowed to pass. It was thought advisable not to precipitate action, but to allow the freebooters to retire to rest.

The men seated themselves in perfect stillness on the grass and on stones. On the inner face of the enormous pile of combustibles lay Rossignol on his bed.

The night was without wind. Not a leaf stirred—there was not even a whisper among the short grass—only the continuous twitter of the crickets and, now and then from far below, yet audible at that height, the croak of a bullfrog in a backwater of the Vézère.

The sky had been overspread with clouds, which had rendered the night one of pitch blackness; but these dissolved. Whither they went was inexplicable—they were not rolled away by the wind, but appeared to evaporate, and let the stars shine through. Then, in the starlight, the valley below became visible, and the river gleamed up, reflecting the feeble light in the sky.

A low-lying fog formed in the valley of the Beune, and lay upon the spongy level, like a fall of sleet.

Jean made a sign; he was again thrust forward over the edge of the cliff, and remained for some minutes looking down and listening.

Then slowly, with upraised hand, he made the requisite signal. He was hastily drawn back.

"All is still," he said. "The fire is nearly out."

"Then the other fire shall be kindled!" said one of the men.

"Nicole!" said Jean. "A brand."

The man addressed went to the charcoal-burner's heap. A thrill ran through the throng. All rose to their feet; even the mutilated man on the mattress lifted himself to a sitting posture.

Silently the men moved between the faggots and the wall of loose stones they had raised, each armed with a stout pole.

Jean put a cow-horn to his mouth and blew a blast that rang into the night as the blast of Judgment. Instantly the rocks and stones were levered over the edge, and instantly the brand, spluttering and blazing, was put into the hand of Rossignol.

It was fitting that he should light the pyre—he who had most suffered. That was why he had been borne to the head of the cliff.

Rossignol drove the flaming torch into the mass of vine-faggots, and instantly up leaped the flame. It ran aloft in the mass, licked and lighted the tallow, it caressed, then exploded the casks of tar, and the whole pyre roared as a beast ravening for its prey.

And its prey was given it.

With their forks, with staves, the whole flaming, raging mass was cast over the edge after the avalanche of stones had been discharged.

[1] *The rock castles on the Vézère and the Dordogne all bear traces of having been burnt. History is silent, but tradition among the peasantry is very precise. They state that it was they who, at the close of the Hundred Years' War, ridded themselves of the Free Companies, and that they did it by the means described in this chapter.*


CHAPTER XI

THE TEN CROSSES

Ogier Del' Peyra , with a much larger body of men, murderously, if not well, equipped, had left Ste. Soure an hour after the departure of Jean. The Vézère makes a great sweep to meet the Beune, but, as though disgusted at the insignificance of its tributary, after having received its waters, it at once turns and flows in an almost directly opposite direction, leaving a broad, flat tongue of land round which it curls, a tongue of rich alluvial soil, interspersed with gravel that is purple in autumn with crocus, and in summer blue with salvia.

Here the party, headed by Ogier, waited in patience till the signal flashed thrice from the heights opposite, when it was immediately answered by three corresponding flares of dry grass.

Then Ogier and his men, under cover of the darkness, moved up the river to the ford, waded across the water, and cautiously crept along the river bank among the osiers in straggling line, till they had reached a suitable point below the "Church." From this point they could see the lights from the windows of that unhallowed edifice shining before them, half-way up the sky like stars, but stars of lurid hue.

Then they sat down in the dewy grass and waited. Hour passed after hour. The stars before them waxed faint and went out.

Then, suddenly, bringing all to their feet, came the peal of the horn, echoed and re-echoed from every cliff, and followed by a crash and a flare.

The scene that ensued was one such as none who witnessed it had ever had a chance of beholding before, or were likely to see again.

The immerse pile of brushwood and fat and other fuel caught with rapidity and rose in a burst of flame high up, as it were in mid-heaven, followed immediately by its being poured over the lip of the precipice, the molten, blazing tar, the incandescent fat, streaked the cliff as with rivers of light, fell on the projecting roof, ran in through the interstices created by the fall of stones that had shivered the covering tiles, and set fire to the rafters they had protected.

Dense volumes of swirling red smoke, in which danced ghostly jets of blue flame, rolled about the habitation of the robber band, and penetrated to its interior. It broke out of the windows in long spirals and tongues, forked as those of adders.

The rocks up the Vézère were visible, glaring orange, every tree was lit up, and its trunk turned to gold. The Vézère glowed a river of flame; clouds that had vanished gathered, crowding to see the spectacle, and palpitated above it.

"Forward!" yelled Ogier, and the whole party rushed up the steep ascent.

For one reason it would have been better had they crept up the steep slope before the horn was blown, so as to be ready at once to burst the gates and occupy every avenue. But Ogier had considered this course, and had deemed the risk greater than the advantage. To climb the rubble slope without displacing the shale was impossible; to do so without making sufficient noise to alarm the sentinel was hardly feasible in such a still night. This might have been done in blustering wind and lashing rain, not on such a night as that when the bullfrog's call rang down the valley and was answered by another frog a mile distant.

The ascent was arduous; it could not have been made easily in pitch darkness; now it was effected rapidly by the glare of the cataract of falling fire and of blazing rafters.

In ten minutes, with faces streaming, with lungs blowing, the peasants reached the gate-house. They beat at it with stones, with their fists; they drove their pikes at it, but could not open it.

Then a man—it was one of those who had been taken and confined in the castle—bid all stand back. He buckled on to his feet a sort of spiked shoe, with three prongs in each sole, and held a crooked axe in his hand.

"I have not been in there for nothing," laughed he. "I saw what they had for climbing walls, and I've made the like at my forge."

Then he went to the wall, drove in the end of his pick, and in a moment, like a cat, went up from stone course to stone course, till he reached the summit of the wall, when he threw aside his foot-grapnels and leaped within. In the panic caused by the sudden avalanche of stones and fire the sentinel had deserted the gate. The oak doors were cast open, and the whole body of armed men burst in.

They found the small garrison huddled together, paralysed with fear, all their daring, their insolence, their readiness on an occasion gone. They stood like sheep, unable to defend themselves, and were taken without offering any resistance.

The surprise was so complete, the awfulness of the manner in which they were visited was so overwhelming, that the ruffians did not know whether they were not called to their final account, and whether their assailants were not fiends from the flaming abyss.

It had come on them in the midst of sleep when stupefied with drink.

"Follow me!" ordered Ogier, and he led the way through fallen flakes of fire, smouldering beams, and smoking embers, to a portion of the castle that was intact. It consisted wholly of a cavern faced up with stone, and the cataract of fire had not reached it, or had not injured it.

"Bring the prisoners to me," said Ogier. "Where is the Captain? Where is Le Gros Guillem?"

The head of the band was not taken.

"Disperse—seek him everywhere!" ordered Del' Peyra.

The men ran in every possible direction. They searched every cranny.

"He has escaped up the ladder to the Last Refuge!" shouted one. The Last Refuge was the chamber excavated above the projecting roof of the castle, cut in the solid rock.

"He cannot," said another, "the ladder was the first thing to burn. See, it is in pieces now."

"If he be there," scoffed a third, "let him there abide. He can neither get up nor down."

"I do not think he is there. He is in Hell's Mouth."

This Hell's Mouth was the tortuous cavern opening upon the ledge of rock occupied by the castle.

"If he is there, who will follow him?" asked one.

"Aye! who—when the foul fiend will hide him."

"I do not believe it," said one of the men who had been confined in the "Church." He indicated with his finger. "There is a mal-pas yonder; he has escaped along that."

A mal-pas, in fact, exists in many of these rock castles. It consists of a track sometimes natural, often artificially cut in the face of the cliff, so narrow that only a man with an unusually steady head can tread it; often is the mal-pas so formed that it cannot be walked along upright, but in a bent posture. Often also it is cut through abruptly and purposely to be crossed by a board which he who has fled over it can kick down and so intercept pursuit.

"Bring up the men for me to judge them," said Ogier, "and you, Mathieu, give me your sharp-pointed pick."

The man addressed handed the implement to his Seigneur, who seated himself on the floor of rock with his legs apart and extended.

"Giraud!" said Ogier, "and you, Roland, run out a beam through one of the windows—through yonder, and one of you find rope—abundance. How many are here?"

"There are twelve," was the answer.

"That is well; twelve—enough rope to hang twelve men, one after another from the window."

Sufficiency of rope was not to be found.

"It matters not," said Ogier. "There are other ways into another world than along a rope. They shall walk the beam. Thrust it through the window and rope the end of it."

"Which end?"

"This one in the room, to hold it down."

A large beam, fallen from the roof in the adjoining chamber, and still smoking and glowing at one end, was dragged in, and the burning end thrust out through a window. The driving it through the opening, together with the inrush of air to the heated apartments, caused the red and charred wood to burst into light; it projected some ten feet beyond the wall, fizzing, spurting forth jets of blue flame over the abyss.

"Number one!" shouted Ogier. "Make him walk the rafter. Drive him forward with your pikes if he shrinks back."

One of the ruffians of the band, his face as parchment, speechless in the stupefaction of his fear, was made to mount the beam, and then the peasants round shouted, drove at him with their knives and pruning-hooks, and made him pass through the window.

There were three men seated on the end of the beam, which rested on a bench in the chamber.

The moment the unhappy wretch had disappeared through the window, Ogier began to hew with his pick into the floor.

"Forward! He is hanging back! He clings to the wall! Coward! He is endeavouring to scramble in again!" was yelled by the peasants, crowding round the window to watch the man on the charred and glowing beam end.

"Drive him off with a pike! Make him dance on the embers!" called one within, and a reaping-hook, bound to a pole, was thrust forth.

A scream, horrible in its agony, in its intensity; and those seated on the beam felt there was no longer a counterpoise.

Chip, chip, went Ogier.

Presently he looked up. He had cut a Greek cross in the chalk floor.

"Number two!" he ordered.

Then the wretch who was seized burst from his captors, rushed up to Ogier, threw himself on his knees, and implored to be spared. He would do anything. He would forswear the English. He would never plunder again.

Old Del' Peyra looked at him coldly.

"Did you ever spare one who fell into your hands? Did you spare Rossignol? Make him walk the beam."

The shrieking wretch was lifted by strong arms on to the rafter; he refused to stand, he threw himself on his knees, he struggled, bit, prayed, sobbed—all the manhood was gone out of him.

"Thrust him through the window," said one. "If he will not walk the beam he shall cling to it."

The brigand's efforts were in vain. He was driven through the opening. In his frantic efforts to save himself he gripped the rafter, hanging from it, his legs swinging in space.

"Cut off his fingers," said one.

Then the man, to escape a blow from an axe, ran his hands along, put them on glowing red charcoal, and dropped.

Chip, chip! went Ogier. He had cut a second cross.

"Number three!" he said.

The man whose turn came thrust aside those who held him, leaped on the beam, and walked deliberately through the window and bounded into the darkness.

Chip, chip! went Ogier. He worked on till he had incised a third cross in the floor.

Thus one by one was sent to his death out of the chamber reeking with wood-smoke, illumined by the puffs of flame from the still burning buildings that adjoined. Ten crosses had been cut in the floor.

"Number eleven!" said Ogier; and at that same moment his son Jean entered at the head of those who had ignited and sent down the cataract of fire that had consumed the nest.

"What are you doing, father?"

"Sending them before their Judge," answered Ogier. "See these ten crosses. There are ten have been dismissed."

Then the man who had been brought forward to be sent along the same road as the rest said—

"I do not cry for life; but this I say; it was I, aye, I and my fellow here, Amanieu, who provided the hundred livres, without which the seven would not have been set free."

"You provided it?"

"Aye, under the Captain's daughter. It was we who did it. If that goes to abate our sentence—well."

"Father, spare these two," pleaded Jean.

"As you will, Jean; but there is space for two more crosses. Would—would I could cut an eleventh, and that a big one, for the Gros Guillem."

Then murmurs arose. The peasants, their love of revenge, their lust for slaughter whetted, clamoured for the death of the last two of the band.

But Jean was firm.

"My father surrenders them to me," he said.

"Then let them run on the mal-pas," shouted one of the peasants.

"Good!" said the brigand Roger; "give me a plank and I will run on it, so will Amanieu."

Ogier looked ruefully at the crosses.

"'Tis a pity," said he. "I intended to cut a dozen."

If the visitor to the Église de Guillem will look, to this day, rudely hacked in the floor, he will see the ten crosses: he will see further—but we will leave the rest to the sequel.


CHAPTER XII

THREE CROSSES

No sooner had Noémi left l'église than with her teeth she tore the red cross off her left shoulder in an ebullition of wrathful resentment.

She rode, attended by the two servants of the Tardes, to La Roque Gageac without speaking.

Her mind was busy. It was clear to her that she could not remain with her aunt after that affair at the Devil's Table. The Bishop of Sarlat was not an energetic ruler; he might demur to making an expedition against Domme, doubt the expediency of attempting reprisals against so terrible a man as Le Gros Guillem, and all for the sake of a Jew, but he could hardly allow her, who had been the mover in the robbery, to remain in one of his towns. It would not be well for her to compromise the Tarde family. She must go to her mother at Domme.

On arriving at La Roque, she told Jacques and Jean Tarde what she had done.

Jacques burst out laughing. "Well done, Cousin Noémi! I am glad our money has gone to some good purpose."

She flushed to her temples. Jean del' Peyra had not welcomed her with commendation. He had received what she had done in an ungracious manner. She resented this. She was bitter at heart against him. That was the last time she would move a finger to help a Del' Peyra.

Noémi remained the night and part of next day at La Roque. Though young and strong, she was greatly tired by the exertion she had gone through, and by the mental excitement even more than the bodily exertion. The distance to Domme was not great. She had but to cross the Dordogne a couple of leagues higher in a ferry-boat and she would be at the foot of the rock of Domme. This rock may be described as an oval snuffbox with precipitous sides, flat, or nearly so, above, with, however, one end somewhat elevated above the other. On this superior elevation stood the castle or citadel. On the lower was the town, uniformly built, with a quadrangular market-place in the midst surrounded by arcades, and every street cutting another at right angles, and every house an exact counterpart of its fellow.

The garrison kept guard on the walls, but their headquarters were in the castle, where also resided their Captain, Guillem. Access to the town was to be had by one way only, and the gate was strongly defended by salient drums of towers. The castle had a triple defence of river, wall and half towers, and possessed a great donjon, square and machicolated. In 1369 it had stood a siege by the English for fifteen days, and had repelled Sir John Chandos and all his force. Since then it had fallen into the hands of the English through the neglect of the French crown to provide the necessary garrison.

Noémi was attended as far as Domme by her cousins' servant. On reaching the town it was at once manifest that something unusual had occurred which was occupying the minds and tongues of the townspeople. The men were gathered in knots; the arcaded market-place was full of them.

The girl entered the castle and proceeded to her mother's room. This lady was past the middle age, finely framed and delicately featured, still beautiful, but languid and desponding. She greeted her daughter without impulsive affection.

"Noémi," she said, "something has happened to discompose your father. I do not know what it is, the whole place is in commotion."

"I will go see," answered the girl.

"I do not think he wishes to be disturbed," said the lady, and sighing, leaned back in her seat.

Noémi at once proceeded to the chamber usually occupied by Guillem, and she saw him there, seated at a table, gnawing his nails.

The insolent, dauntless freebooter was much altered. He sat with his elbows on the table, his fingers to his teeth, his hair ragged, his tall, smooth head, usually polished, without its wonted gloss, his eyes staring stonily before him.

The Captain was mortified rather than hurt. He had been driven like a wolf athwart the woods by the peasants; smoked out of his lair by Jacques Bonhomme, like a fox.

He had escaped from the "Church" by the skin of his teeth. Roused by the crashing in of the roof, then by the flood of fire, he had sprung from his bed, half-clothed, without his jerkin and boots, had seized his sword and had fled. In an instant he had realised the impossibility of resistance, and had run along the mal-pas, and, selfish in his fear, had kicked down the plank over the chasm to secure himself from pursuit, though at the sacrifice of his men.

He had lurked at a distance, watching his blazing castle and then had run on. Occasionally he had all but rushed into the arms of peasants flocking from the neighbourhood. Once, in the grey morning light, he had been recognised and pursued, and had only saved himself by cowering under an overhanging stone till the men had gone by.

Bootless, running over rocks and stones, and these latter in many cases flints that were broken and cut like razors, his feet had been gashed, and he had at length been hardly able to limp along. Prickles of briar, spines of juniper, had aggravated the wounds, and it was with extreme difficulty that he had reached the Dordogne, seized a boat, and rowed himself across into territory nominally English. Even then he had not been safe. He knew it. He must reach Domme before the tidings of the disaster arrived, or all the subjugated country would be roused. He broke into a farmer's stable, took his horse, and galloped with it up the valley, nor halted till he reached the gates of Domme, where his warder opened to him in amaze to see the governor of the town, the captain of the garrison, arrive in such a deplorable condition.

Since his arrival, after he had bathed his feet and had them bound up, he had been seated at his table, gnawing his nails, glaring into space, his heart eaten out with rage, humiliation, and raven for revenge.

To have been defied by a Del' Peyra! To have been warned by his adversary and not to have profited by the warning! Guillem's bald forehead smoked, so hot were his thoughts within him.

Noémi stood looking at the Captain, amazed at the change that had come over him—at his haggardness, at his stoniness of eye.

"Father, what has happened?"

"Go away! I want no women here."

"But, father, something has taken place. All Domme is in commotion. The streets are full."

"Full!" in a scream; "talking of me—of my disgrace! Call my lieutenant; I will send the pikemen through the streets to clear them—to silence the chattering rogues."

"But what does this all mean, father?"

"Come here, child." He waved his arm without looking at her. She obeyed. She stepped to his side and stood by the table.

"Father, your fingers are bleeding; you have gnawed them."

"Have I? It matters not. My feet are bleeding, my brain is bleeding, my honour is bled to death."

"What has happened?"

He took her hand. The only soft part in this terrible man was his love for Noémi, and that was rarely shown.

"What are the Del' Peyras to you?" he asked roughly.

"Nothing, father."

He looked round, caught her steady eye, winced, and turned his away.

"So—nothing. Why did you then ransom these men?"

"Because, father, I had pity for the men themselves."

"Why?" He could not understand this simple, natural, elementary feeling. She did not answer him, but loosened her hand from his; she took the torn strips of red silk that had formed her cross and put them on the table before him. "I renounce my companionship," she said.

He did not regard her words or her action.

"I am glad the Del' Peyras are nothing to you. I swear—" He sprang up but sank again. He could not bear to stand on his mangled feet. "I swear to you, I swear to all Périgord I will root them out; I will not leave a fibre of them anywhere. I will let all the world know what it is to oppose me."

"What has been done, father?"

Again he turned his face, but could not endure her clear eyes.

"I cannot tell you. Ask others."

Steps were audible in the anteroom, and Roger and Amanieu entered. They saluted.

"Captain," said Roger, "we only are come."

"And the others?"

"Ten of them—made to leap the beam."

"Yes, Captain, and the Seigneur del' Peyra sent his compliments to you, and was sorry your legs were so long. You'll excuse me, Captain, they were his own words; he made me swear to repeat them. He was very sorry your legs were so long. He cut ten crosses in the stone, one for each of the comrades, and, said he, there was room for another, and he'll do you the honour of making its legs long also, if he has the chance of catching you."

Guillem gnashed his teeth; the blood rushed into his eyes. He glared at the messenger.

"I think, Captain, you might have left us the plank," said Amanieu. "As it was, we had to borrow one from the peasants."

"Send me the lieutenant. This can only be wiped out in blood!" roared the Gros Guillem, in spite of his wounded feet, leaping into an upright position. "I care not that I am lamed—I care not—I shall be lifted into my saddle. I will not eat, I will not sleep till I have revenged myself and the murdered ten, and my burnt castle and this outrage on my honour."

"I am here, Captain," said the lieutenant, stepping forward. He had entered along with the returned companions. In the blindness of his agony of mind and rage Guillem had not noticed him.

The filibuster turned his face to the lieutenant. It was terrible. His red but grizzled hair, uncombed, shaggy with sweat, electrified and bristling with the fury that was in him, his pale eyes and red suffused balls, his great mouth with pointed fangs, the lower jaw quivering with excitement, made his appearance terrible.

"Lieutenant!" shouted Guillem; "call out all the men available—all but such as must remain to guard the castle and this cursed disloyal town, in which every citizen is a traitor. Muster them outside the castle; bring forth as many horses as we have. If I am carried, I will go. At once, before these peasants have recovered their astonishment, because they surprised us when we were asleep: at once, as swiftly as possible, to chastise them. Cut down every peasant in arms: give no quarter, but above all, take me Ogier del Peyra. I will pay fifty livres for him—to any man—to have him taken alive. I do not desire him dead; I must have him alive. Do you mark me? First of all, Del' Peyra. At once, before they expect reprisals—at once."

His hand was on the table. In his fury he shook it as if it had been his enemy he was grappling.

"To horse, Roger and Amanieu, and revenge your wrongs, as I will revenge mine."

"Pardon me, Captain," said Roger. "What is this I see? the red silk cross—what? has she taken this off and renounced companionship? So do I. I cannot serve against the father Del' Peyra or the son who spared my life." He plucked at the cross on his shoulder, then with his dagger unripped it, tore it, and threw it on the table.

"Nor I," said Amanieu surlily, "not because they spared me, but because you kicked down the plank." And he also tore off his cross and flung it on the table.

CHAPTER XIII

THE END OF L'ÉGLISE GUILLEM

The exultation of the peasants at having taken "the Church of Guillem" would have resulted in a sack and insubordination but for two causes: one, that the spoil of the robbers had not been recovered; and the other, the great firmness of Jean del' Peyra and his father.

The pillaged goods must be found. None had much hesitation in saying where they were. Everything worth preserving had been stowed away in the rock-hewn chamber above the castle, in the face of the cliff, and this was now very difficult of access.

The roof of the castle from which it was reached was broken in, portions had been consumed, other portions were so charred as to be dangerous.

The peasants had begun to throw down the walls, to demolish every portion of the structure that was artificial, but Jean stayed them.

"If you do this," said he, "how shall we reach the treasury above?"

The day had broken but the sun had not yet risen. The slope below the Church and the Church itself presented a strange spectacle.

The incline was strewn with smouldering fragments of wood, of faggots, the bind of which had been burst by the flames, and had released sticks that had not been ignited, of rafters from the castle blackened by the fire, of long streams of pitch that had fallen and run and had ceased to flame. In the midst of the road by the river-brim stood a cask on its bottom, emitting volumes of black smoke. Amid the wreckage lay the corpses of the men who had been made to leap to their death. When daylight came, it was perceived that one alone had not died instantly. He had been seen to stir an arm and raise his head, and a peasant had run down and dispatched him.

The face of the cliff, wherever reached by the flames, had become decomposed. Chalk will not endure the touch of fire, and the white, scaly surface had flaked off and exposed yellow patches like sandstone. Scales, moreover, were continually falling from the blistered scar.

A portion of the floor of the main chamber of the castle that projected beyond the face of the cliff remained unconsumed, and sustained the beams of the wall that formed the screen in front. Many of the stones that had been inserted between the rafters had fallen out; nevertheless, sufficient remained to make it possible for an agile man to reach the charred and ruinous roof.

"Let some go to the cliff-edge overhead," said Jean, "and tie the end of a rope to a tree, and let it down in front of the chamber in the rock. Then I can, I believe, climb to it, and see! I will thrust this piece of torn red silk through the roof at the end of a pike, as a token where to lower the cord."

An hour elapsed before the rope end with a heavy stone attached to it came down through the shattered roof. This was now left hanging, and Jean del' Peyra began to climb. He bade the men undo the stone as soon as he was aloft, and in its place attach a large basket to the cord, which he would draw up and fill with whatever he found in the chamber. Knowing, however, how little the peasants could be trusted, he required his father to keep guard, and take possession of what he lowered, the whole to be retained undisturbed till each could claim his own goods, and of those unclaimed a distribution would be made later among such as had assisted in taking the stronghold.

Nimbly as a cat Jean ascended among the beams. He had to use extreme caution, as some of them were smoking, and he had to beware of putting his hand on fire that was unobservable by daylight, and of resting his foot on cross pieces that had been reduced to charcoal. The stones shaken by him as he mounted, and loosely compacted among half-burnt beams, and themselves split and powdered with heat, came down in volleys; but as this portion of the castle overhung the precipice from seven to ten feet, they did not jeopardise those who were in the cavernous part of the chamber.

Jean rapidly swung himself to the rafters of the roof, and, after testing which would bear his weight, crept along one till he touched the cord. Then, by this aid, he was able to creep up the face of the rock, that, however, came down on him in dust where crumbled by the heat; and in a couple of minutes he was in the cave.

A rapid glance round assured him that it was untenanted, and that it contained all the booty that had been accumulated by the routiers in many excursions.

In lockers cut in the native rock, and furnished with wooden shelves, were gold chalices and reliquaries of Limoges enamel, silver-tipped drinking-horns, and a richly bound volume of poetry, the interminable metrical romance of Guerin de Montglane. In chests were silks and velvets; in boxes the jewellery of ladies. Besides these costly articles were many of inferior value, garments, boots, gloves, caps, of every sort and quality. Of money there was not much, save one bag that contained a hundred livres—it was the ransom of the seven men, the plunder of the Jew Levi.

As soon as Jean had passed everything down to the men below by means of his basket, that travelled frequently up and down, he took hold of the rope and easily swung himself to the rafters, and let himself down into the chamber of the castle. Here his father had disposed of the booty in parcels, and had arranged that all was to be carried down the hill and deposited in the Church of Ste. Soure, where division would be made in three days' time. Then every claimant should be satisfied. Those sacred vessels which had come from churches would be restored to the churches, and notice would be issued to all sufferers in the country round to come and retake whatsoever they could show was legitimately their own.

"And now, father," said Jean, "it seems to me that we are but at the beginning of our troubles. We have taken this outpost and destroyed a handful of our oppressors. But behind this stands Domme, and in it is a garrison. The Captain has slipped through our fingers. He will never consent to abide without an attempt to recover what is lost and to revenge his humiliation. It is my advice that we utterly destroy this castle, so that it can never be occupied again. Then, that we should send out spies to observe the movements of the enemy, and report if he be on his way to make reprisals. Lastly, that we hold ourselves in readiness to encounter him when he sets forth. Let us choose our own ground, and that is half-way to success."

"You are right, Jean," said the old man. "We will take council at noon and prepare. Now, lads! down with the walls, rip up the floors, down with everything! Remember this—a first advantage is a sure prelude to a final disaster unless followed up. Do you know why we have taken and destroyed this 'Church'? Because the ruffians had surprised us and made easy spoil at Ste. Soure. They sat down here to eat and drink and lay down to sleep in full confidence that we were overawed. Now we have surprised them. Take care lest what chanced to them chance also to us. At noon meet in the Ste. Soure church. Now to work. Down with the rest of the twigs of this vultures' nest!"

With a cheer the men set to work to demolish the castle that had so long menaced the country. There were many willing hands employed, and the work was already half done; it needed little more than some shaking to throw the entire structure to pieces. Only here and there was there solid wall; that here and there was where there was solid shelf on which to build. Elsewhere all was wooden framework filled with stones.

Thus was L'Église Guillem destroyed. At the same time some great thing was won. The people, spasmodically, had exerted its power, and had acquired consciousness of its strength; it held up for a moment the head that had been for so many centuries bowed under the feet of its tyrants. It had looked military power in the face, and had not winced.

## CHAPTER XIV

### THE BATTLE OF THE BEUNE

Le Gros Guillem, at the head of fifty men, was on his way to chastise the peasants of the Vézère Valley.

The number he had with him was not large, but he was unable to spare more for this expedition. A sufficient garrison must be left in Domme. Besides, to deal with peasants, a handful of soldiers with steel caps and swords was certain to suffice; hitherto it had sufficed, and that at all times. What was Del' Peyra? He had never distinguished himself in feats of arms; no one had ever heard that he had taken them up at any time. The dung-fork and the ox-goad befitted him. It was said he had more than once ploughed his own land.

The men were mounted so as to make the chevauchée as rapidly and effectively as possible, without allowing those whom they were resolved to attack time to bestir themselves and assemble to offer resistance. If these Ste. Soure peasants did learn that the ribauds were coming they would flee to the rocks and hide themselves there. That they should attempt resistance was not to be anticipated. Guillem had determined to burn every house in the village, to devastate the fields, cut down all the fruit-trees, and try whether fire and an escalade would enable him to capture Le Peuch, the stronghold of the Del' Peyras, so that he might be able to punish the chief offender, the Seigneur Ogier, as well as all his retainers and vassals.

The Captain alone was silent and immersed in gloomy thoughts. The rest of the Company were merry and indulged in banter. They were bound on an expedition of all others best to their liking.

As they descended the valley of the Little Beune they passed under the rock of Cazelles, and looked up with a laugh at the peasants who were peering out of the holes of the cliff, much like jackdaws. Not a bullock, not a sheep was left in the valley. The houses were deserted, and probably everything that could be carried away had been transmitted to the cave refuges.

"Look!" mocked one of the riders. "The fellows had such a scare the other day at Ste. Soure that these villains at Cazelles have not yet recovered confidence."

Where the Little Beune unites with the Great Beune the blended calcareous waters ooze through bog in a dreamlike, purposeless manner round a shoulder of rock that is precipitous, but which has a sufficiency of solid ground at its feet to allow of a practicable way being carried over this deposit.

The Beune and the Vézère are like two different types of character. The latter never deviates from the direction it has resolved on taking except when opposed by obstacles impossible to overleap, and these it circumvents. It saws down every barrier it can; it never halts for a moment; if it turns back in the direction it has been pursuing it is solely that it may seek out a channel more direct and less tortuous. It is so with men and women who have a clear conception of an object at which they are aiming, some purpose in their lives.

With the Beune it is otherwise. It has no perceptible current; it does not run; it has no flow; it slips down. It finds itself in a channel and drifts along from one stagnation to another; it has had nothing whatever to do with the formation of its channel. It does not even lie in a bed of its own making. It is a bog and not a river—here and there spreading into pools that wait for an impulse to be given them by the wind, by the whisk of a heron's wing, to form the ripple that will carry some of its water over the calcareous bar it has itself raised by its own inertness. No one could say, looking at the Beune, in which direction it was tending, and it does not seem to have any idea itself. Its sluggishness accumulates obstacles; marsh grass is given time to throw out its fibrous roots, and reeds to build up hurdles across the stream, and the cretaceous particles settle at leisure into walls obstructing it; consequently diverting it. It lurches stupidly from side to side and then listlessly gives up every effort of advance. We stoop to drink of the Vézère. We turn in disgust from the Beune.

On each side of the Vézère as it swings along is alluvial soil—beds of the utmost richness that laugh with verdure, where the hay harvest is gathered thrice in the year. In the equally broad valley of the Beune is no pasture at all, nothing good, nothing but profitless morass. Where the waters touch good soil they corrupt it. The crystal waters of the Vézère nourish every herb they reach; the turbid ooze of the Beune kills, petrifies all life that approaches it.

Is not this also a picture of certain characters? Characters!—save the mark! Characterless individuals that we have seen, perhaps have to do with, whom we avoid when possible.[2]

[2] Within the last five years a determined effort has been made to reclaim the valley of the Beune. To do this, a channel has been cut for the river, that has to be incessantly cleared.

Hardly had the band of routiers turned into the main valley, and the foremost men had reached the cliff, before a horn was blown, and at once a shower of stones was hurled from above the horsemen.

At the same moment they saw that the road before them was barricaded. Trees had been felled and thrown across the track, and from behind this barricade scowled black faces and flashed weapons.

Some of the horses reared, struck by the stones; some of the riders were thrown to the ground. The horses, frightened, bounded from the road. They could not turn, being pressed on by those behind; they rushed away from the shower of stones into the level track of valley-bed on their right, and at once foundered in the morass. There they plunged, endeavoured to extricate themselves, and sank deeper. The semi-petrified fibres through which their hoofs sank, held to their legs, and prevented the beasts from withdrawing them. After a few frantic and fruitless efforts they sank to their bellies and remained motionless, with that singular stolidity that comes over a beast when it resigns itself to circumstances which it recognises it has not the power to overcome.

The men who had been carried into the marsh threw themselves off. The routiers were wiser than were the knights at Agincourt. They did not overburden themselves with defensive armour which would weigh them down and render them incapable of movement. Most of their clothing was of leather, with but a little steel over their breasts and shoulders. With agility they threw themselves from their sinking horses, and waded to the hard ground. At times they floundered deep, but were able to throw themselves forward and where the surface was most precarious, advanced like lizards, till they reached ground where the rushes showed that it was sufficiently compact to sustain them upright.

Meanwhile, those in the rear who had halted when the first ranks were broken and dispersed hesitated what to do. To push forward was to incur the same fate, and their pride would not suffer them to retreat.

The Captain was behind. He was suffering greatly. His wounded feet had begun to inflame; they were swollen and tortured by the compression of his boots. He could not bear to rest his soles on the stirrup-irons. To rise in his stirrups and hew with his great sword, as he had purposed, was impossible. The pain he endured fevered his blood, churned his anger to frenzy, which this unexpected check did not serve to moderate.

He had his wits about him, however, and he saw that those who held the rock must be dislodged or no advance could be made.

Accordingly, he ordered a party of his men to dismount, peg their horses, and ascend to where the peasants were threatening them with their piles of stones.

This could be done—at all events attempted—from the lateral valley, where the slope was moderate and densely overgrown with coppice.

Bitterly now did the leader regret that for a second time he had underrated the spirit and the sagacity of his opponents. He ought to have marched at the head of a larger contingent or have postponed his attempt till a more suitable opportunity presented itself.

With his usual effrontery, Guillem had ridden across country by the shortest way, through the lands of the Bishop of Sarlat, instead of descending the Dordogne to the junction of the Vézère, and then ascending the latter river to Ste. Soure.

He had not done this for two reasons—one was that the formidable Castle of Beynac, in French hands, blocked the passage down the Dordogne; the other was that he had measured and properly appreciated the incapacity of the prelate: he knew the Bishop had not the men at his disposal to send to contest his passage.

At this time his real danger lay, as he very well knew, in tidings of his ride reaching the Castle of Commarques, hardly an hour's distance up the valley of the Great Beune. This was a dependence of Beynac, and was held for the French king.[3] What garrison was there he knew not, but it was certain to be small. Nevertheless, even a small band of troopers or experienced men-at-arms assailing him in rear while engaged in bursting through this barrier of peasants before him might be more than dangerous, it might prove disastrous.

*[3] This splendid ruin—one of the finest in Périgord—has been recently purchased by the Prince de Croye, who is engaged in cutting and constructing roads to it, with the purpose of restoring the castle as a residence. A charming residence it is likely to prove to such as are mosquito-proof.*

Resolved at all hazards to dislodge those on the height, he sent his lieutenant up the steep hillside at the head of his trustiest men, or, rather, as many of these as he could spare without breaking the ranks directly opposed to those who watched and menaced from behind the barricade.

But the task of storming the height was one that was difficult. Not only was the party sent up it inadequate in numbers, not only were the assailants inconvenienced by the steepness of the ascent, but their weapons were not calculated to be effective in a tangle of chestnut, rowan, and sloe laced about with ropes of bramble and clematis. They carried swords; they were unprovided with pikes; whereas those who held the height were armed with knives fastened to long poles, which they could thrust with excellent effect at the men who were attacking. Time was expended in the scramble; and the assailants were exhausted before they came within sight of the eyes of those they were sent to dislodge. In the brushwood the routiers could not keep together; the many sprays shooting up from stumps of felled chestnut separated them. They had to hack their way through the tough chains of clematis, and they were lacerated by the thorns of the sloe-bushes and the teeth of the wild rose and blackberry-briar. They could not come to a hand-to-hand fight. Their enemies calmly waited, watching them in their struggle, and drove at them with their blades through the bushes, forcing them to spring back to avoid death.

It took some time for the lieutenant in command to realise that he had been dispatched on a task which he was incompetent to achieve. But when he had determined this, he bade his men desist and retreat to the valley below.

They had not retreated far on their way down before they saw that the aspect of affairs below was greatly changed since they had started on their scramble.

Behind the barricade had been ranged the charcoal-burners with their forks, under the command of Ogier del' Peyra.

These had remained covered by their breastwork, expecting the enemy to make a second attempt to advance along the road. When, however, this was not done, and they saw them drawn up motionless, and shortly after heard the shouts and cries from the height, then Ogier recognised that the line of men before him was covering an attack on his son, who held the rock.

He at once gave the signal to advance at a rush. With a shout of joy the charcoal-burners burst over the barricade and charged along the road, led by the Seigneur, and fell upon the double line of troopers.

A furious hand-to-hand mêlée ensued. The horses were alarmed by the sable figures with black faces and hands who sprang at them, and recoiled, not only from the sight, but also at their smell, producing disorder. The struggle that ensued was hand to hand. No quarter was asked and none was given. The routiers were borne back, several had fallen, but also many colliers rolled on the ground.

At this juncture, down from the hill, out from among the coppice leaped the contingent that had failed to capture the height. It arrived at the most critical moment, just as the horsemen were struggling to disengage themselves and fly. They came upon the colliers in rear, they stopped accessions to their ranks from behind. Now their blades served them well, and the rout that had begun was arrested.

The arrival of this body of men startled the peasants. They did not understand whence they had sprung; and they retreated.

"Turn! Back to Domme!" yelled the Captain.

The men recovered their horses, remounted, and still fighting, began the retreat.

As they came under Cazelles a shower of projectiles was launched upon them from above.

The peasants gave over the pursuit. They were incapable of keeping pace with the horses.

And now, as they fell back, down from the height came Jean del' Peyra with his men.

"Where is my father?" he asked eagerly, and looked round.

Old Ogier was nowhere to be seen.

"Search among the fallen!" ordered Jean in great alarm.

Every dead and dying man was examined.

Then came back a charcoal-burner, hot, for he had been running, and the sweat streaming over his face had washed it into streaks, like those that stain the face of the chalk cliffs.

"What—the Seigneur?" asked the man. "He is taken."

"Taken!"

"Aye, taken and carried away by the rouffiens."


CHAPTER XV

A THREATENED HORROR

When Gros Guillem returned to the Castle of Domme, his feet were so swollen that the boots had to be cut off, and his feet swathed in linen.

By his orders, Ogier del' Peyra was thrown into a dungeon for the night. The old Seigneur had been surrounded, disarmed, and captured by some of the routiers while recovering their horses, which Ogier was endeavouring to prevent by cutting their reins.

As soon as he was taken he knew that his doom was sealed, and he bore the knowledge with his usual stolidity, amounting to indifference. A quiet, plodding, heavy man he had ever been, only notable for his rectitude in the midst of a tortuous generation; he had been roused to energy and almost savagery by circumstances, and, thus roused, had manifested a power and prevision which no one had expected to find in him. Now that all was done that he could do, he slid back into his ordinary quietude. He slept soundly in his prison, for he had greatly excited and tired himself during the day.

"Man can die but once," he said; and the saying was characteristic of the man—it was commonplace. This was, perhaps, less the case when he added, "An honest conscience can look Death in the face without blushing."

Consequently, when thrust into his dungeon, he took the blanket ungraciously afforded him, and wrapped it round him, ate his portion of bread, drank a draught of water, signed himself—said the peasant's prayer, common in Quercy and Périgord as in England—

Al let you mé coutsi
Cinq antsels y trobi:
Doux al capt, trés as pès,
Et la mayré de Diou al met.

Equivalent to our "Four corners to my bed; two angels at my head; two to bottom; two to pray; two to bear my soul away."

Then he threw up his feet on the board that was given him for bed, and in five minutes slept and snored.

It was otherwise with Le Gros Guillem. He would tolerate no one near him but his wife and daughter, and they came in for explosions of wrath. The fever caused by pain had inflamed his head: he talked, swore, raged against everyone and all things, and boasted of the example he would make on the morrow of the man who was in his power. Noémi knew that some expedition had been undertaken, and that it had failed, but she knew no particulars, certainly had no idea that it had resulted in the capture of Jean del' Peyra's father.

She bathed and bound up her father's feet, and applied cold water as often as they began to burn. This gradually eased him, especially as he lay with his feet raised. The wounds he had received were of no great depth, but they were painful, because the soles of the feet are especially sensitive; and as all the grit and thorns had been removed by the surgeon before he left Domme, there was no fear but that with rest he would be well again in a week or ten days; well enough at least to walk a little.

The wife of Gros Guillem was a dreamy, desponding woman, who paid no attention to what he said, interested herself in no way in his affairs; neither stirring him to deeds of violence nor interfering to mitigate the miseries wrought by him. She accepted her position placidly. She was fond of Guillem in her fashion without being demonstrative, and it was a marvel to everyone how it was that he was so attached to her, and that she had maintained her hold on him through so many years.

It was reported, and the report was true, that the lady had been carried off by Guillem from the Castle of Fénelon. Guillem had retained her, in defiance of the excommunication launched at him by the Bishop of Cahors, and in defiance of the more trenchant and material weapons wielded against him by the Fénelon family, which was powerful in Quercy, and had a fortress on the Dordogne above Domme, and a house and rock castle above La Roque Gageac, side by side with that belonging to the Bishop of Sarlat. In an affray with Guillem's company the husband had been killed; the widow accepted this fact as she had accepted the fact that she had been carried off by violence. She sighed, lamented, pitied herself as a veritable martyr, and acquiesced in being the wife of the man who, though he had not killed her husband with his own hand, had caused his death.

With morning Guillem was easier and his head cooler, but there was no alteration in his resolve with regard to Del' Peyra. He would deal with him in such a signal manner as would from henceforth deter any man from lifting a finger against himself.

In his fever he had racked his brain to consider in what manner he would treat him.

He sent for his lieutenant and ordered that he should himself be carried into the keep.

"And," said he, "bring up the prisoner—and call up the men, into the lower dungeon."

Noémi was walking on the terrace of the castle that same morning; she had been up late, had attended to the fevered man, her father, and now was sauntering in the cool under the shade of the lime-trees, clipped en berceau, that occupied the walk on the walls—a walk that commanded the glorious valley of the Dordogne, that wondrous river which flows through some of the most beautiful and wild scenery in Europe, and is also the most neglected by the traveller in quest of beauty and novelty.

At this time she knew something of the events of the previous day. She knew also of the taking and the destruction of l'Église Guillem. Twice had the Del' Peyras measured their strength against the redoubted Captain, and twice had they forced him to fly. At the head of raw peasants without rudimentary discipline they had defied and beaten the troopers of a hundred skirmishes. She was not surprised. She had seen Rossignol. Great wrongs wake corresponding forces that must expend themselves on the wrong-doers. It is but a matter of time before the thunder-cloud bursts. Every crime committed sends up its steam to swell the vaporous masses and carries with it the lightning.

Nursed though Noémi had been in an atmosphere of violence, hearing of it as matter for exultation, the ruin of households and homesteads spoken of as a matter of course, she had never been brought face to face with the wreckage till she was shown it at Ste. Soure.

And did she feel anger against the Del' Peyras for having taken up arms to revenge their wrongs? Nothing was more natural: nothing more just where the Crown and law were powerless, than that men should right themselves. She would have despised the Del' Peyras had they sat down under their wrong without any attempt to repay it.

Noémi's nature was a good one, but it was undisciplined. Her mother had allowed her to go her own way. Her father treated her with indulgence, and that precisely where she should have been checked.

In a lawless society she had learned to fear neither God nor the king. Both were too far off. The one in Heaven, the other in England; too distant to rule effectively. A certain perfunctory homage was claimed by both, neither was regarded as exercising any control over men. A feudal service was all that a bandit in those days, or indeed any baron or seigneur, thought of rendering to the Almighty. He would fight in a crusade for Him, he would do knightly homage in church, but he would no more obey the laws of the Christian religion than he would those of the realm of France.

Noémi had seen but little of Jean del' Peyra, and yet that little had surprised her, and had awoke in her thoughts that were to her strange, and yet, though strange, consonant with her instinctive sense of what was right and wrong.

Jean del' Peyra not only surprised her, but occupied her thoughts: she saw, almost for the first time, in him one of a different order from the men with whom she had been thrown. Even her cousins, the Tardes, were akin in mind and consciencelessness to the routiers. What they did that was right was done rather out of blind obedience to instinct, or allegiance to their feudal lord, the Bishop of Sarlat. They were noble, for they had escutcheons over their doors, but all their nobility was external. They were boastful, empty roysterers.

On the other hand, the Del' Peyras were quiet, made no pretence to being more than they were, and were inspired with a moral sense and a regard for their fellow-men.

She saw how far greater was the influence exerted by the old man and his son than was exercised by that remorseless man of war, Guillem, or the braggart Jacques Tarde. Her father controlled men by fear; Ogier del' Peyra moved men by respect. The Captain was a destructive, and only a destructive element. Solely by means of men like the Del' Peyras could human happiness and well-being be built up.

Noémi was a thoughtful girl.

At first, somewhat contemptuously, she had set down Jean del' Peyra as a milksop; from what she had heard, his father was but a country clown. But the country clown and the milksop had revealed in themselves a force, an energy quite unexpected. Noémi laughed as her busy mind worked. She laughed to think of the discomfiture of professional fighting men, accustomed to arms from their youth, by a parcel of inexperienced peasants and charcoal-burners.

She was glad that these oppressed beings had risen. It showed that there was in them a nature above that of rabbits. She had seen a thousand times the holes into which they ran at the glint of a spearhead, at the jangle of a spur. But now they had issued from their holes and had hunted like wolves.

But these poor, ignorant timid peasants would never have done this had they not been led. It was the moral character, the true nobility of the Del' Peyras that had rallied the people around them, given them courage, and directed their blind impulse of revenge into proper forms of retaliation.

Was the execution of those ten men of her father's band to be accounted a wanton act of cruelty?

Noémi could not admit this. Some such rude administration of justice was rendered necessary by the times. The men who had suffered had merited their death by a hundred deeds of barbarity.

It was as though a spell had fallen on the girl. She was exultant, her heart was bounding with pride, and that because her father and his ruffians had been put to rout by their adversaries.

The girl was unable to explain to herself the reason of this, but, indeed, she did not admit to herself that it was as has been described. Yet she was sensible that some spell was on her. She had proposed to cast one on Jean. That kiss she had given him had been intended to work the charm. But, alack! there are dangerous spells which a witch may weave that affect herself as much as her victim, and of such was even this.

As Noémi paced the terrace, her mind in a ferment, she was accosted by Roger, the good-natured, somewhat impudent fellow who had attended her on her expedition to the Devil's Table.

He had torn off his red cross, but he had not left Domme, nor, indeed, the castle. He would no longer share in an expedition against Ste. Soure, but he was not unwilling to do any other service for the Captain.

He could now exult over his comrades who had returned from such an expedition with diminished numbers, defeated.

He approached the girl and accosted her.

Noémi answered curtly that she did not desire to speak to him. She disliked the forwardness of the man.

"But," said he, "I would save his life—he saved mine."

"Save whom?"

"The Seigneur del' Peyra."

"What of him?"

"He was taken yesterday."

"The Seigneur—taken!"

"And the Captain is now with him—in the dungeon under the keep."

"Doing what?" asked Noémi in breathless alarm.

"There is none in the world can save him but yourself; the Captain would listen to no one else."

"Save him—from what?"

"The oubliette."


CHAPTER XVI

VADE IN PACE

The thought of undefined horror conveyed by that word "oubliette" for a moment held Noémi as though it had paralysed her. But this was for a moment only, and then she bounded in the direction of the keep.

A word must be said as to what an oubliette was. In almost every mediæval castle in France and Germany the visitor is shown holes, usually in the floor, that descend to a considerable depth, and which are said to be oubliettes—that is to say, places down which prisoners were dropped when it was to the interest of the lord of the castle to sink them in oblivion.

Sometimes these places communicate with a river or a lake, as at Chillon, and this passage is set with irons, presumably to cut in pieces the body of the man cast down it.

In the vast majority of cases these so-called oubliettes are nothing but openings connected with the drainage of the castle or else are the well-mouths of cisterns in which the rain-water from the roofs was collected and stored.

Nevertheless, the fact that skeletons have been found in some of the closed subterranean vaults, and that a percentage of them cannot be explained as having been anything else but receptacles for prisoners thrown in, to die a languishing death, and lastly, the historic certainty that some poor wretches have so perished, shows that popular belief is not wholly unfounded. The writer has himself been let down by ropes into one in which four skeletons were entombed, and it is well known that in 1403 one of the Counts of Armagnac so disposed of his cousin, who lingered on thus immured for eight days. The son would have shared his father's fate but that out of horror at the notion of being flung down the well on the corpse of his father, the poor lad dropped dead on the brink.

Moreover, under the title of vade in pace, the oubliette was used, not in castles only, but in convents as well, and was there introduced by Matthew, Prior of St. Martin des Prés, in Languedoc, in the middle of the fourteenth century, when the Archbishop of Toulouse interfered to forbid the employment of this inhuman mode of execution. A prelate might step in to check the barbarity of a prior, but who was there to hold the hand of a noble?

Noémi saw a cluster of men outside the door that led into the dungeon, and forced her way through them. The dungeon was not large, it would not admit more than a dozen men. It opened on to a platform of rock on the outside of the castle, not into the inner court. Access to it was obtained by a doorway in the basement of the keep, where the wall was ten feet thick. The chamber was vaulted, and only near the middle sufficiently lofty to admit of anyone standing upright in it. There was no window by which light and air could penetrate. When the door was shut, both were excluded. The walls, the floor, the vault were of square-cut limestone.

At the further end, immediately opposite the door was a recess, conchoidal, and in this recess what seemed to be a well. There was a stone step in the floor, and above that a circular coped wall, precisely such as may be seen where there is a well; with this difference, that the orifice was not two feet in diameter, a very inconvenient size for a bucket to pass up or down.

In the dungeon sat Le Gros Guillem on a pallet, with his feet raised and bandaged. Before him, bound, with his hands behind his back, was Ogier del' Peyra, between two jailers. The old man had concluded that his head would be struck off, at the worst that he would be hanged. The sight of the vade in pace, and the knowledge that he was to be cast down alive and left to a lingering agony, had blanched his cheek, but did not make him tremble.

Ogier did not know, he could not guess, the depth of the oubliette. But he was aware that such were sometimes not so profound but that he who was flung in broke some of his bones, and thus died of a combination of miseries. Happy he who, falling on his head, was reduced at once to unconsciousness.

"Well, Del' Peyra," cried Guillem, in his harsh tones, rendered harsher by the feverishness and weariness of the past night, "will you not stoop to beg of me your life?"

"It is of no use," answered Ogier.

"Hold the lights, that I may see him!" ordered the Captain.

Two of his men brought torches that emitted as much smoke as light. In the dungeon, darkened by the men crowding the door, artificial illumination was necessary.

"You are right there!" shouted Guillem, in response to the words of Ogier. "I shall not spare your life. But what think you of the mode of death? Come, kneel, kiss my foot—wounded through you; and I may consent to have you hanged instead of thrown down yonder!" He indicated the well-like opening.

The glare of the torches was on Guillem's face as much as on that of his prisoner. He was haggard with pain and mortified pride. He was but half-dressed, was in his shirt, and his shirt was open over his red, hairy breast. His tall, polished head shone like copper in the lurid flicker of the links. His great mouth, half open with a grim laugh, revealed the teeth, pointed as though to bite and tear. He was very thin, but muscular, and his limbs were long. As already said, it was but in jest that he was entitled "Le Gros."

It may be questioned whether in the heart of a single ruffian present there stirred the smallest emotion of pity for the man who was to be sent to so horrible a fate, for all had been humbled by Ogier, and all angrily resented their humiliation. Moreover, all desired to avenge their ten companions.

"Hold up the light, that I may see how he relishes it!" ordered Guillem, brutally. Then he said: "Pull off his boots, strip him to his shirt."

But immediately he countermanded the order.

"Nay," said he, "leave him his leather belt and boots; he may satisfy his cravings on them. And, Sieur Ogier, when you want more leather, call for my boots. They have been cut to pieces, and are useless to me. They may make a meal for you."

The Captain looked steadily at his victim from under his lowering eyebrows.

"How came you to think of resisting me?" he asked.

Ogier shrugged his shoulders.

"This execution will be noised everywhere," continued Guillem. "I shall take care of that. And then every man will have a wholesome dread of me, and a fear of resisting me."

"Not my son Jean," retorted Ogier.

"Your son Jean comes next," said the Captain. "I shall deal with him presently."

"You must catch him first," said Ogier.

"Take the prisoner to the hold!" shouted Guillem.

Then the two jailers laid their hands on the shoulders of Ogier del' Peyra.

"You need not drag me. I can walk," said the old man.

Those crowding the close and narrow dungeon fell back, as well as they were able, to make a passage for the condemned man.

He was taken to the well-mouth and seated on it, with his face towards the door, through which glimpses of sunlight were visible athwart the heads that filled the opening. Ogier had been divested of his jerkin. He was in his shirt and breeches and boots. As the Captain had bidden that his belt should be left him, this had been refastened about his waist, after that his coat had been removed. In order to divest him of his outer garments it had been necessary for the jailers to remove the handcuffs that had fastened his arms behind his back.

"Cursed smoke!" said Guillem. "We are smothered in the fume. Stand aside all of you and let the fresh air enter, that we may breathe. Hearken, Ogier! Will you yet ask life of me?"

At Guillem's command the men had stepped forth and completely cleared the entrance, so that the brilliant sunlight flowed in as well as the pure air. And this light fell directly on the man who was soon to be excluded for ever from it. He was seated on the well-mouth in his white shirt. His face was as grey as the thick hair of his beard. He was conscious that he was looking for the last time at the light. He could see intense blue sky, and one fleecy cloud in it. He could see the green turf, and some yellow tansies standing against a bit of wall in shade, the tansies in full sunlight; and he could see a red admiral butterfly hovering about them. It was marvellous how, with death before him, he could yet distinguish so much  But he looked at everything with a sort of greed, because he saw all these things for the last time. For the first and only moment in his life he saw that a red admiral was beautiful, that the sky was beautifu , the grass beautiful.

"You have not answered me," said Le Gros Guillem, sneering. "Messire Ogier, will you yet ask life of me?"

"If you were in my hands, as I am in yours, would you ask that question?"

Le Gros Guillem paused one moment. Then with an oath—

"No!"

"Nor I of you," said Ogier gravely.

Guillem raised his hands. The fingers were inordinately long and thin. He made a sign to the jailers, one of whom stood back, on each side of Ogier, by the well-mouth, with his hand on the shoulder of the prisoner. Each man, as was customary, had his face covered—that is to say, a black sack was drawn over his head, in which were two holes cut, through which peered the eyes.

"Throw him down!"

At that moment, taking advantage of the avenue made for the admission of air, Noémi rushed in. A couple of men stepped forward to intercept her, but she was too nimble for them; she was within almost as soon as they thought of throwing themselves in her way, and had cast herself upon Ogier and clasped him with her arms.

"Father! Father! It cannot, it shall not be!"

The door was filled again; the men crowded in to see what new turn events would take, whether this intervention would avail.

The jailers desisted as they were raising the old man; they felt that the sight of the execution of the sentence could not be permitted to a young girl. Moreover, she held Del' Peyra fast, and he could not be extricated from her arms without the exercise of force.

"Noémi!" exclaimed Le Gros Guillem, throwing his feet off the pallet, "what is the meaning of this? Why are you here? At once away! Do you hear me?"

"I will not let go! He shall not die! Father, it cannot—it shall not be!"

"Unloose her arms," ordered Guillem, and signed to the men.

Firmly they obeyed. It was in vain that the girl clung, writhed, endeavoured to disengage her arms from their grasp, and clung to the condemned man. They held her like a vice and drew her back from the pit-mouth and interposed their persons between her and the man she was endeavouring to save.

Then, in a paroxysm of horror and pity, Noémi threw herself on her knees before her father and implored him to yield.

"What is Del' Peyra to you?" he asked sternly.

"Nothing—nothing," she gasped. "Oh, father, let him go! let him go!"

"Twice have you interfered between me and him. Why is that?"

She could not answer his question; she did not attempt to do so. She persisted in her entreaties. In her anguish she caught hold of one of his injured feet and made him cry out with pain.

"Father! If I have ever done anything for you! If you have any love for me—any thought to do what I wish—grant me this. Spare him! Spare him!"

"Never!" answered Le Gros Guillem. Then he waved his long hand and said, "Remove this silly girl."

But when Noémi felt hands laid on her, she leaped to her feet, shook herself free, and said, panting—

"Let be! Do not touch me! I ask his life, no more."

"You do well, child," sneered the Captain. "You then run no more risk of disappointment."

"Yet—if that be denied me, there is one thing I do ask," gasped Noémi.

Her breath came as though she had been running up hill. She put her hands to her head, and held it, till she had recovered sufficiently to proceed.

"There is one thing I do ask," she repeated. "Do not cast him down—let him down gently."

A harsh laugh from Le Gros Guillem.

"You are a silly child, a fool, who know not what you ask. You will prolong his torture, not shorten it—but you shall have your wish. Be it so."

He waved to the jailers.

"Go, child, go!" said he to his daughter.

"I will stay and see it done," she said. "I will not ask another thing."

She stood erect and looked at the old man; her mouth quivered, and her eyes were as though fixed hard in their sockets like stones in a setting.

And the sight was one to freeze the blood.

The jailers raised Ogier, who offered no resistance, but fixed his eyes strainingly on a spot of light above a man's head in the doorway.

He was lifted till his feet were above the well, and then he was let down by ropes passed under his arms, slowly, deliberately.

Those holding the torches raised them, and the smoke described cabalistic devices on the roof. The glare was on the sinking man.

He went down below his knees, then his waist disappeared. Involuntarily he put forth his arms to arrest his descent, by gripping the well-breast, but recollected that resistance was in vain, and lowered his arms to his sides.

Then his breast was hidden, then his shoulders went under. For a moment all visible was the ghastly grey face with the glittering eyes, and then—that also was gone.

He uttered no cry, no groan, he went down like a dead man, into profound darkness, into his living tomb.

All was still in the dungeon, save for the labouring breath of those who looked on. The jailers lowered till the ropes became slack. Then they knew the poor wretch was on the floor of the vault below. Each man threw down one end of his rope and drew at the other, even as at a funeral the ropes are withdrawn when the dead has been lowered.

In the stillness, Guillem laughed—silently—showing all his fangs, and waving his arms in the direction of the oubliette mouth, and extending his lean fingers said—

"Vade in pace!"


## CHAPTER XVII

### IN THE RAVEN'S NEST

When Le Gros Guillem was carried back to his room, he said to his wife, "Where is Noémi?"

"I believe—that is, I suppose she is going to her Aunt Tarde at La Roque. She said something about it. Something has occurred and she is not herself. I don't know what it is."

"I dare say!" laughed the Captain. "Noémi has witnessed this day what has been seen by few girls. She stood it manfully—at the last."

"I dare say. I know nothing about it," said his wife.

"If she is going to La Roque, then Roger and Amanieu shall accompany her. I have a letter to transmit to Ste. Soure."

He sent for writing materials, and wrote in a scrawling hand:

"Dear and most valiant friend, Seigneur Jean del' Peyra at Le Peuch Ste. Soure.—Please you to know that your father is let down into oblivion. Dear and well-loved Sir, God have you ever in guard.

"Written at Domme, Wednesday, and sent by the hands of Roger and Amanieu."


That was the fashion of epistolary correspondence as conducted in those times. "Dear friend" was the salutation to a deadly foe, "God have you ever in guard," when the writer would like to cut the throat of him he addressed.

Such was the letter received by Jean del' Peyra. It was not explicit. He had been in the greatest anxiety relative to his father. That he would be put to ransom was his hope, but not his expectation.

He looked to the bearer of the epistle for explanation, and then for the first time saw Noémi, her face rigid and ghastly, as though she had seen a ghost, and could not shake off the impression.

"Jean," she said, "let them go back. I will tell you all, between you and myself. No, not back. Step aside."

When Noémi saw that she and Jean were alone she said—

"Do you not understand? Your father—he has been let down into an oubliette."

Jean started back as though he had been struck in the face by a mailed hand.

"And now," proceeded Noémi, "there is but one chance for him, one way open to you."

"Where—where is it?" gasped the lad.

"At Domme. No, you cannot storm that castle. It has held out against French and English, and it would hold out against your peasants."

Jean looked at her in silence. What other way was open?

"You must go yourself to Domme," she said.

"And entreat for my father? We will sell all—land, castle, seigneury—all!"

"That will not suffice. The Captain would take you and cast you in where lies your unhappy father."

"Then what do you mean?"

"You must take me."

"Along with me—to Domme?"

"No, take and confine me here."

"I do not understand."

"I can—I saw it. I saw it at once when I was in that horrible place, when my father refused to listen to me and I pleaded for him. Then I saw clearly there was no other chance for his life."

"And that is—?"

"That you put me into the same position."

"What, in an oubliette?"

"Put me in a dungeon, and threaten unless your father be restored, and back here safe by sunrise to-morow, that you will cast me down as he has been cast down."

"We have no oubliettes here."

"You have precipices."

Jean looked in astonishment at the girl.

"See, Jean!" she said, and a dark spot came in each cheek, "by no other way can you rescue your father than by going before him—I mean my father, and threatening that unless your father be released immediately, you will have me put to the same horrible end."

"Never!"

"It must be."

"It would never be done—never."

"Listen to me, Jean. You must have me imprisoned here. Place guards over me and go to my father fearlessly. Say to him that the instant the first spark of the sun lifts over yon hill"—she pointed to the heights opposite—"if the Seigneur and you are not here to stay their hands, you have told your guards to throw me down."

"If I were to threaten it, it would not be done."

"Yes, it would. Do you suppose that your peasants here and your armed men would spare me if they knew that their Seigneur and his son had both been sacrificed by Le Gros Guillem? They would tear me to pieces. The women would stab me with their bodkins. I had rather be dashed down the cliffs than that."

The young man remained silent, considering. The girl's proposal did give him a hope of recovering his father; the threat, which he did not for a moment entertain the thought of executing, might, perhaps, force the routier captain to surrender his prey.

Noémi plucked a ring from her finger and extended it to Jean.

"I see," said she, "you will yield. Take this as token to my father that I am here, as sign that your menace is not an idle one. Now lead me away."

In the congeries of precipitous cliffs, like teeth, that rise above Ste. Soure and go by the name of Le Peuch, one possesses a rock-refuge of a peculiar character. To reach it a steep ascent has to be effected up an almost vertical piece of rock, in which places have been cut for the feet. This climb gives access to a grassy ledge. If this ledge be pursued, a buttress of crag is reached that completely blocks the terrace. But this has been scooped out, like a carious tooth, into a chamber or guard-room. It is entered by a door artificially cut, and he who explores the place there finds himself in an apartment with a window dug through the face looking south, and with sheer precipice below it. At the back are seats cut in the stone.

Immediately opposite the entrance is another door, communicating with another ledge, which, however, does not extend more than ten feet, and ends in steep cliff. Along the face of this cliff holes have been scooped for the reception of the feet, so that a man can walk along the front of the rock till he reaches a projecting mass like that he has traversed, and this mass is excavated into a series of chambers.

This rock-refuge is one that could not be taken, if only moderate precautions were observed. The man who passed in the socket-holes for his feet to the door of the first chamber scooped out in the scar must traverse in front of a window, through which it would suffice for a child to thrust his hand to touch him to upset his balance and send him headlong below to certain death.

There was no place better calculated to serve as a prison than this Raven's Nest, as it was called. Jean was by no means sure that what Noémi said might not come true; if the peasants learned who she was, they might take advantage of his absence literally to tear her to pieces, for they were greatly exasperated at the loss of their master, the old Seigneur. If he were to leave the girl for some hours at Le Peuch, she must not only be protected against an attempt at recapture, but against the resentment of his own people, who might lose their heads when they found that he as well as his father was lost to them. A woman like Rossignol's wife was a firebrand inflamed with unslaked lust for revenge. A few words from her might set all in movement. The Southern Gauls are an impulsive, excitable, and, when excited, an unreasoning people. The routiers had not spared their wives and daughters, why should they scruple about reprisals on the daughter of their deadliest oppressor?

Distressed as Jean was at his father's fate, the fear of what might happen to Noémi if left alone at Le Peuch for a moment overbore his filial distress.

"You must follow me," he said; and he beckoned to the two men who had attended her to accompany him as well.

Without further words he led them up the ascent, along the ledge, and into the guard-room.

There he said to Amanieu and Roger—

"Your Captain's daughter is going to remain yonder." He pointed across the gulf to the rock chambers in the projecting mass of cliff. "I shall not be at Ste. Soure to protect her. You know what these people are. Even you are not safe, though my father granted you both your lives. As I see, you no longer bear the brand of lawlessness. Do not concern yourself about what takes me away. I leave you here in guard of her. Let no one approach. Yonder, in those retreats, there is always a supply of food, in case of emergency. There is water also. You need not enter for that. She will pass to you what you require through the window. Keep guard here for her sake and for your own, till I return." Then to Noémi he said, "Dare you follow me?"

"I!" she said, and almost laughed. "Have you forgotten the stair to the Bishop's Castle?"

Jean stepped off the platform, and walked along the face of the rock and was immediately followed by the girl, without the least misgiving or giddiness.

On reaching the door cut in the crag on the further side, Jean stepped in.

These rock chambers are cool in summer and warm in winter. There was no well here dug in the heart of the rock. Probably owing to its height above the level of the Vézère—some 300 feet—it had not been thought likely that a vein of water would be tapped; so the atmospheric moisture was caught by little runnels scored in the rock, and all these runnels led into a receiver, in which there was generally to be found a supply of water, though not a great quantity. Each window was provided with shutters, and doors fitted into the entrances, and could be fastened. Beds were scooped in the rock, arched above, and these couches were strewn with heather and fern. In cupboards cut in the walls were stores, to be used in case of necessity.

When Jean had shown the girl everything, he held out his hand.

"Noémi!" he said, and his voice shook, "good-bye! We may never meet again. But do not think that harm would be done you by me—even if the worst were to happen!"

"Jean!" she answered gravely, and went to the doorway, and looked down. "Do you think that anyone who fell here, who tripped coming along these steps, who stumbled at the threshold, would not be dashed to pieces in an instant?"

"I am sure he would. That is what affords you protection here."

"I do not mean that, Jean." She refrained from speaking for a moment. He put out his hand to her, and she took his. Both their hands trembled.

"Jean, I shall watch for the sunrise from the little window. If you and your father have not returned—"

"Then we shall both perish together in the oubliette."

"Yes—and the moment the sun comes up—"

"Noémi—what then?"

"The moment I see the first fire-spark—"

"Noémi!" He feared to hear what she was going to say.

"Yes, Jean, I shall throw myself down—here."


CHAPTER XVIII

IN THE DEPTHS

Before that Jean del' Peyra ventured to cross the Dordogne and approach Domme, he fastened a white kerchief to his cap, as token that he came on peaceful errand, as bearer of a message. As such he was received within the walls, and was conducted to the castle, and given admission to the vaulted hall in which lay Le Gros Guillem on his pallet with his feet up.

The long, lean, pale-faced man looked hard at him when admitted, and said—

"Who are you?"

"I am Jean del' Peyra," answered the lad, and cast his cap with its white appendage on the table.

"Jean del' Peyra! and you venture here!" roared the Captain. "You must in verity be a fool!"

"I came—trusting to that," said the youth with composure, pointing to the white token.

"Then you came trusting in vain. I regard it not."

"Perhaps you will regard this," said Jean, extending the ring, which he plucked from his little finger.

The Captain looked at the signet, started, and brayed forth—

"That belongs to Noémi! How came you by that? You have murdered her."

"I have not murdered her. If she dies it will be through you. She is my captive."

"I do not understand."

Le Gros Guillem slipped his feet from the pallet to the floor. He could not walk, he could not even stand, as his feet were swathed in rags.

"It is not difficult to enlighten your understanding," said Jean. "You sent away your daughter with two men as her guard. They are all in my power. They are at Le Peuch. Their fate—that is to say, hers—depends on you."

"So—you war against girls!"

"If we do violence to the young and feeble, from whom have we learned the lesson but from you and your ruffians?"

"You know what I have done to your father," said the freebooter, malignantly. "I will do the same to you."

"And the same fate will befall your daughter—at once," said Jean, decidedly.

The Captain was staggered. He was uneasy. He said sullenly: "For what purpose have you come here?"

"For this," answered Jean. "With your own hand you have let me know where my father is. Unless he be released, and allowed to return with me to Le Peuch, your daughter will perish miserably."

Jean went to the window. The Captain looked suspiciously after him.

"The sun is setting," said the young man. "In an hour it will be gone. Unless before he reappears in the East, unless, to the moment of his rising, my father and I are not returned to Le Peuch safe and sound, it will be too late. Your daughter saw what was done to the old man—what think you of a like fate for her?"

"I do not believe she is in your hands. She is at La Roque."

"Send to La Roque, if you will, and inquire—only remember that will take time, and time is precious. We must be back at Le Peuch before the first spark of the sun reappears, or the deed will be done. Your daughter will be dead."

Le Gros Guillem's face became ashy grey with alarm and rage, commingled with embarrassment.

"Besides," said Jean with composure, "look at the ring. You know that it is taken from her finger."

The Captain turned the ring about in his hand. Then he struck the table with his clenched fist and screamed—

"Outwitted! outwitted again! The devil is fighting for you!"

"Rather is he deserting you to whom you sold yourself," retorted Jean.

The chief remained sullen, with knitted brow and clenched teeth, brooding.

"The sun is set," said Jean, and pointed through the window.

The yellow flame had disappeared that had flushed the hills on the further side of the Dordogne, the wooded slopes and the tall rock of Vitrac, itself a natural fortress.

The Captain moved uneasily on his pallet, and looked furtively at his guards near the door.

Jean read his thought.

"Nothing you can do is of any avail, save the release of my father. The first ray of sun that lights the sky sees the spark of life die out in your Noémi's heart."

"What guarantee have I that you will not play me false, and refuse to give her up?"

"My word, my honour, and that of my father. Send men with me if you will. Only remember now that time is winged and is flying."

With a horrible oath, Le Gros Guillem again struck the table and called to the guards. They approached.

"Take him"—he indicated Jean—"take him to the oubliette chamber," said he; "let cords down, release the man, and let both go as they will."

He flung Noémi's ring on the table, and cast his maimed feet on the pallet once more, and clenched his teeth and knitted his red brows.

Jean took up the ring and said: "I will return this to her."

The guards now conducted him to the keep. Lights were provided, also cords; the door into the cell was opened; and with a shudder Jean entered.

Snatching a torch from one of the men, he went to the breastwork of the well, and leaning over it, let the torch flare down the abyss.

"Father!" he cried; "my father!"

Then he paused for an answer.

There was none.

With the link he endeavoured to illumine the depths below, but found that this was not possible. He could see nothing save an awful blackness, in which the rays of the torch lost themselves, without illumining any object.

"Father!" again he cried.

This time he heard a sound—an inarticulate groan.

"Let me down. I must go to him," said Jean.

"You cannot take a light with you," said one of the men.

"You can carry one down unlighted, and kindle it when you are below," said a second.

Jean saw that it was as the men said. The orifice and throat of the well were so narrow that he must descend without holding a burning light. He nodded, and slipped his arms through the loops in the cords.

"Give me a candle," said he, and one was immediately handed to him.

Then he seated himself on the well-breast, with his feet hanging down inside; and when the men were ready, thrust himself off.

Jean was lowered gradually down the bottle-throat, till all at once the sides fell away, and he was swinging in space. The effect of being suddenly plunged in absolute blackness of darkness is not so startling as some might suppose. The retina of the eye carries with it an impression of light; and as Jean was let down through void space of absolutely rayless gloom, it seemed to him as though a rosy halo attended him; he could, indeed, discern nothing—no object whatever—but he could not suppose that he did not. All at once his feet touched ground. Then he released his arms, and struck a light with steel and flint. Some time elapsed before the tinder kindled, and from the tinder he was able to ignite the candle. Jean's hand shook. He was nervous lest he should see his father dead or dying. It seemed inexplicable to him that he was not answered readily when he called. Finally, the yellow flame flickered. Then the lad raised the candle above his head and looked about him. He was in a dungeon some thirteen feet square, built of hewn stones in large blocks, laid together with the finest joints, that did not show mortar. The sides were perfectly smooth. The chamber was arched overhead; there was in it no door, no window, no hole of any sort save that in the midst of the vault overhead, through which he had descended.

The description of the interior of the oubliette is in accordance with that into which the author was lowered at Castelnau le Bretenoux. The ruin of the castle at Domme is so complete that the oubliettes there, if they existed, are buried.

Against the wall, lying with his head raised, his eyes open, looking at the light, not at Jean, was his father, his legs extended on the cold floor, and about him were strewn the bones of dead men, skulls and skeletons, more or less disturbed by the blind groping of the last victim.

Jean at once went to the old man.

"Father! dear father!" he said.

"Eh?"

"It is I—Jean."

"Eh?"

"I have come to release you."

"Eh?"

The old man's senses seemed lost.

Jean at once knelt, and drawing a phial from his breast, poured into Ogier's mouth a spirit distilled from the juniper berries that grow on the Causse.

His father drew a deep inspiration.

"It is a long night, and a bad dream," he said. "Where are the tansy and the butterfly?"

"Father, no time is to be lost. Can you rise?"

The old man scrambled to his feet. He was as one in a trance. Jean led him to the cords, and thrust his father's arms through the loops.

"Mind and hold your hands down," he said. "Father, you will see the light of day! the light of day! Be quick! you will see it before it is gone."

"The light—the sun?" asked Ogier, eagerly.

"The sun is set, father; but you will see the evening sky and the stars."

"The light! O my God! the light, do you say?"

"Draw him up!" ordered Jean, and watched with great anxiety as the ropes were strained and the old Seigneur's feet left the ground. Then Ogier was carried up, and passed with head, then shoulders through the orifice in the vault.

It seemed to Jean as though half an hour elapsed before the ropes descended again. When he saw them fall, then he eagerly blew out the candle, and committed himself to the cords. In three minutes he was above ground. He saw his father standing in the doorway, looking out over the terrace at the clear evening sky, drawing in long breaths of the sweet pure air of evening into his lungs.

Jean turned to the two men.

"I thank you," he said. "Here is gold. If I can do aught to repay you, in the many troubles and changes of affairs that occur, it shall be done. Your name?"

"I am Peyrot le Fort."

"And I, Heliot Prebost."

"Enough! I shall not forget. We must away. Lead me once more to the Captain."

Jean took his father under the arm. The old man walked along with tolerable steadiness, but said nothing. He was as one stupefied. He did not seem to realise that he had been released, but to be labouring under uncertainty whether he were dreaming that he was at liberty or not, and was oppressed with the dread of waking to find himself in the abyss.

Jean and his father were introduced into the hall where lay Le Gros Guillem. The Captain had not allowed lights to be introduced, as his eyes were somewhat inflamed by the irritation which pervaded him.

"Captain," said Jean. "You must remember that this is not all. The day is spent. We must travel all night, and I have a horse awaiting my father. But you have despoiled him of his coat. He cannot leave in his shirt."

"I have not his coat," said Guillem, roughly. "I restore the man, that suffices."

"It does not suffice. Give him back his jerkin."

"The executioner—the jailer has it. It is his perquisite."

"I cannot go after him. Send for it yourself. Consider what you are apt to forget, that time is all-important."

"Here!" ordered the Captain. "Bring the old fellow one of mine—any worn one will suffice."

A moment later a leather coat was given to Jean, brought by a serving-man. It was dark in the hall. Le Gros Guillem did not concern himself to look at what was produced. Probably the serving-man himself had taken the garment in a hurry without regarding it.

As Jean threw the jerkin over his father's shoulders, he felt that it was lined throughout with metal rings, and was impervious to a sword-blow or a pike-thrust.

As Ogier, invested in this garment, prepared to depart, the Captain, with brutal insolence, shouted—

"Seigneur! was it cold and black below?"

The old man did not reply.

"We two have met thrice," pursued Le Gros Guillem. "Once I fell on you at Ste. Soure and made you run," he laughed harshly; "secondly, you fell on me unawares, and I came off the worst. The third time we met on the Beune. It might be esteemed a drawn battle, but as I had captured you, I had got what I wanted. However, I have been over-reached; I am outwitted once more this time. Take care how we encounter for the fourth time. Do you mark me, Ogier del' Peyra? The fourth time—that will be the fatal meeting for one or other of us. The fourth time, Ogier."

"The fourth time. I shall remember," said the old man dreamily, and touched his forehead.

"Lead him away. Peyrot and Heliot, you shall ride with the Sieur and his son to Le Peuch. Stay a moment! a word before you go."

He waited till Del' Peyra and his son had left the hall and were descending to the courtyard. Then he said—

"Attend them till you are at Le Peuch, get my daughter safely into your hands, and then cut them down—these cursed Del' Peyras—and bring me their heads at your saddle-bows. You shall be paid what you choose to ask."


CHAPTER XIX

A NIGHT RIDE

When Jean del' Peyra with his father and escort arrived at the point opposite the house of the ferryman on the Dordogne he shouted for the boat.

Night had set in, but the moon would rise in an hour; in the meanwhile some light lingered over the sunken sun, and the stars were shining faintly.

The river gliding on in rapid descent, but without rush and coil, reflected the light above. It was as though a heaven of sparks seen through tears lay at the feet of Jean as he stood and waited in vain for the ferry.

He was vexed at the delay. Time was speeding along. His father's condition made him uneasy. The old man was singularly reticent and stolid; he expressed no satisfaction at his release.

After waiting and renewing his shouts to no purpose, one of the men said—

"There is a wedding in this ferryman's wife's family. I have a notion that he may have gone to the merrymaking. It is not often that there are passengers at night that need his punting-pole."

"We must try the ford," said the other.

"Where is that?" asked Jean, impatiently.

"Further down."

"Then lead to it immediately. We have already squandered too much valuable time."

The party now descended the river-bank till the spot was reached where the Dordogne could be traversed without danger by the horsemen.

The beasts went in. There had not been much rain of late, consequently the ford was passable. The water, however, surged up the leg when the horses had entered to their girths.

Then, all at once, Ogier del' Peyra laughed.

"What is it, father?" asked Jean, startled.

"It is not a vision. I am not asleep!"

The old man had been oppressed with fear, lest what he went through was a phantasm of the brain, and lest he should wake to the hideous reality of a living entombment. The swash of the cold water over his foot, up his calf, above his knee, was the first thing that roused him to the certainty that he was really free.

Without difficulty and danger the little party crossed the river; they ascended the flanks of the great plateau and passed at once into oak woods. Thence, after a while, they emerged upon a bald track, where there was hardly any soil at all, and the whole region seemed to be struck with perpetual hoar-frost. The hoe, even the foot turned up chalk-flakes. Nothing could grow on so barren a surface.

The moon rose and made the waste look colder, deader than under the starlight.

Suddenly shouts were heard, and at the same moment before the little party rushed an old grey wolf. As he passed he turned to them with a snarl that showed his fangs gleaming as ivory in the moonlight. He did not stop—he fled precipitately; and next moment from out of a dell rushed a troop of men armed with pikes, pitchforks, and cudgels, attended by a legion of farm-dogs yelping vigorously.

The little party drew up. The moon gleamed on the morions and the steel plates sewn on the buff jerkins, and black to westward on the white causse[4] lay the shadows of horses and men.

[4] The Causse, from Calx, is the chalk or limestone plateau.

A portion of those pursuing the wolf halted. "Haro! Haro!" shouted one man. "Here are human wolves, the worst of all! Let us kill them before we run the other down."

In the clear moonlight they had seen the crosses of the routiers on the arms of the two men sent from Domme. In a moment the party was surrounded, and the two freebooters to protect themselves drew their swords.

Jean pushed forward. "My friends, do you not know me? We are the Del' Peyras, and my father is but just released from bondage. I am taking him home."

"We will not hurt you, Messire Jean," said a peasant. "But these fellows with you—they are beasts of prey. They have killed our men. Stand aside, that we may knock them off their horses and then beat out their brains."

"You shall not do this."

"Why not? They are brigands, and not fit to live."

"They are under my protection."

The peasants were ill satisfied; having felt their power they had become impatient of all restraint on it.

"Look here," said Jean, "my honour and my father's are engaged for these men. Do not force us to draw our swords on their behalf."

"How do you know but that they will fall on you?"

"They dare not," answered Jean.

"I would trust a wolf rather than one of these. Come on!" The last address was to his fellows.

Then those who had halted turned and ran in the track of such as were pursuing the wolf.

What Jean del' Peyra had said was true enough. The two men attending him would not dare to commit an act of treachery on the way to Ste. Soure. He and his father were safe till Noémi was restored.

Jean spoke to his father. The old man was silent as he rode; now he roused himself as from a trance to answer Jean.

"What did you say, my son?"

"Father, we must push on at a quicker pace."

"I cannot push on—I want to go to sleep."

"To sleep, father?"

"I am falling from my horse with fatigue. I must get off. I must lie down. I have not had my proper rest."

Jean was dismayed; time was slipping along, the moon describing her arch in heaven; he must reach Le Peuch before daybreak, and now his father asked for a halt. It was true that he had allowed time for resting the horses on the way, but how long would the old man require for his repose? The strain on his nerves, the horror of the darkness and expectation of a lingering death in the vault, had been so great that a reaction had set in, and he was unable to keep his eyes open.

"Father," said the young man, "you cannot tarry here on the open causse, we must get on, into the coppice, to a charcoal-burner's lodge. There is one at no great distance."

A few minutes later Jean looked at his father. The old man had let fall his bridle, his head was sunk on his breast; in another moment he would have dropped from his saddle.

The youth called to him, and Ogier started and said:

"I am coming—directly."

In another second he was again asleep.

It was needful to dismount and make Ogier walk. So alone could he be kept awake. Half a mile distant was the charcoal-burner's heap, and a rude cabin of branches beside it.

One of the routiers led Ogier's horse. The old man became angry and irritable at being forced to walk. He scolded his son, he complained that he was badly treated; in vain did Jean explain that he desired him to go on but a little way. The Seigneur stood still, and said he must sit down—he could not, he would not proceed.

Then Jean poured the rest of his flask of spirit down Ogier's throat, and said peremptorily, "You shall come on, whether you will or no."

The old Seigneur obeyed, grumbled, and in a few minutes was at the charcoal-burning station, and had flung himself on a bed of fern in the hut, and was asleep almost as soon as he had cast himself on the bracken.

The charcoal-burner recognised Jean del' Peyra and saluted him respectfully, but looked askance at the two routiers.

"Have you seen or heard anything of the hunt?" asked the collier. "My mate has gone with the rest after the wolf. You see that grey beast has already carried off three children. Yesterday it was Mascot's babe—and now all the country is up; and they are going to run the wolf down. There is a ring formed round the causse.They lured him with a dead sheep. It is to be trusted they will kill him."

Jean said a word or two in reply. He was very uneasy. The heaviness with which his father slept showed him that he was in no condition to be roused at the end of the hour and made to remount. Ogier's strength was exhausted, and this was not to be wondered at, considering what he had gone through.

Jean spoke to the collier, and explained to him that he proposed letting the old man remain where he was and sleep his full. He himself must ride on with his companions, and he would return in the morning for his father.

Meanwhile the routiers had drawn aside and were conversing in a low tone.

"What say you, Heliot? The old fellow will not ride on."

"Then one of us must stay, Peyrot," answered the other, "and the other proceed with the young one."

"Why not finish them at once?"

"You fool! We cannot—we must recover the demoiselle first."

"That is true—I will stay—you ride forward."

"It is one to me which I dispatch," said Heliot. "You can remain, Peyrot, and it is well for us that the Seigneur has broken down."

"Why so?"

"Because we should have found it difficult to lay hands on them at Ste. Soure or at Le Peuch, among their own people."

"There will be Amanieu and Roger."

"Yes—Amanieu and Roger; but all depends—if there be only women about the thing will be easy enough, but if men be there in arms, I do not see how we could do it."

"But now—"

"Exactly—now all is coming smooth to our hands," said Heliot. "For the young Seigneur must return hither to fetch his father—and on the Causse, here among the coppice, away from all habitations, we can dispatch them easily."

"I will kill the old man at once—as soon as you have ridden on," said Peyrot.

"As you like—but you cannot reckon on the collier. He is a big man. If you kill him first, well and good; but if he be on the alert, and you note how suspiciously he looks at us, then he may escape and run and give the alarm, so my sword will be prevented taking the fresher blood of the young Del' Peyra."

"Then what would you have me do?"

"Remain here. Disarm the suspicions of the charcoal-burner. Keep near the Seigneur, especially in the morning. If he be awake, be at his side; if asleep, watch by his bed. The collier must attend to his charcoal. When I draw near with the demoiselle and Amanieu and Roger, and the young man, then cut him down and take his head. I will do the same to the youth."

Presently the voice of Jean was heard summoning them to mount. His impatience would not endure a longer delay.

Peyrot le Fort came up and said: "I am not going further."

"Not coming on? You must."

"I cannot; my horse is lame."

"Lame! I did not observe that as we rode along."

"You had no eyes save for your father."

"If lame, of course you must stay. We cannot—we dare not linger here longer. Tarry with my father till we return."

Then Jean went into the booth of the charcoal-burner and looked at his sleeping father. Within was dark, and accidentally he touched the old man's foot. At once Ogier started into a sitting posture, and cried out, "Yes, yes, Guillem! The fourth time—I shall not forget!"

Then he threw himself back, and was sound asleep again.

## CHAPTER XX

### THE RING

Noémi could not sleep that night. She sat in her rocky prison looking out over the valley of the Vézère at the distant landscape bathed in glorious moonlight. Opposite Le Peuch the rocks are not precipitous; there is a falling away of the plateau into soft undulations and stages, rounded in the wood and sombre in their mantle of trees.

The moon was full—so bright that it eclipsed every star save its attendant Venus; the whole sky was infused with light, the darkness of the deep blue turned to grey. The Vézère gleamed as a plate of molten silver below.

The river passed with a sigh rather than a murmur. How white, dazzling white, those cliffs must seem facing the moon, standing up like gigantic horse-teeth! The moon smote in at the window where sat Noémi. It bathed her face, her arm that was raised to sustain her chin.

How glorious was the world! how peaceful! how happy! Only man, with his lust of rapine, his love of violence, transformed it into a place of torment. What if there were no parties—one English, the other French—but all this fair land reposed under a single sceptre! And what if that one sceptre controlled evildoers, put down lawlessness, and, extended over the land, bid it rest! What if all evildoers were rooted out, and first among these Le Gros Guillem!

Below in Ste. Soure was the sound of a human voice, of a woman singing to her child that wept and would not sleep. Noémi could not hear the words, but she knew the air, and with her lips murmured—

B'aqui la luno
Sé y'n abio dios, t'en dounarioy uno!

"Moon, moon! gloriously bright! If there were two I would give thee one! I would give thee one—thee! thee!"

To whom would she give the moon if there were two, and one were at her disposal? The mother would give it to her babe because her whole heart was for that child. And she—Noémi—to whom would she give the moon—to whom?

Was she not going to give something better than the moon—even her precious life?

Yes; not for a moment did she waver in her resolution. If Jean del' Peyra did not return on the morrow by first sun-peep she would cast herself down—and what matter? Would life be worth a rush to her when she knew that Jean was dead? Dead he would be, if he did not return—dead, along with his father—

...B'aqui lo vito!
Sé y'n abio dios, t'en dounarioy lu doui!

"Life! life! precious life! If I had two I would give thee both!"

The night passed slowly, and still Noémi sat at the opening in the rock. The moon had mounted high in heaven and sailed down the western sky. It no longer peered into the rock-chamber, no longer flooded her form as she sat motionless at the opening.

Her brain had no rest. Thoughts turned and twisted in her head. Again and ever again she asked whether for her sake her father would yield up his prey—sacrifice the opportunity offered him of putting his foot down at once on and crushing the Del' Peyra family in the persons of father and son together. She knew the implacability of his temper, the ruthlessness with which when offended he pursued his revenge to the end. Dear she might be to him, but was she dearer than vengeance on such as had humiliated him as he had never been humiliated before? The air became raw and chill, with that rawness and chill which precede dawn.

Noémi rose and went to the door and looked across the chasm to the guard-room, which, it will be remembered, was an excavation in a rocky buttress. Holding the jambs she looked and listened. She could hear no sound. Amanieu and Roger were asleep. They had not been disturbed during the day, and in confidence that no danger menaced, they had cast themselves on the bed and slept. Still holding the jambs, she leaned forward and looked down. Below all was dark. The moon was behind the hill, and its shadow lay black along the slope. There was so much light in the sky that she was able to distinguish in the depths masses of white rock, lying about faintly discernible like high up vaporous white cloud in a summer sky—rocks there on which her head would dash and her limbs be broken within a few hours, unless Jean and his father appeared—white rocks there that would be splashed with her blood. If Le Gros Guillem would not yield up his victims this would be the end of her young life. To him she would, she could not return. Her honour—her word was engaged—here she would perish.

The night was chill, she drew a mantle about her, and resting her head against the stone jamb of the window, looked out dreamily—and slipped into unconsciousness, to start to full life and activity of thought at a sound, the whistle of Roger or Amanieu in the guard-room rock.

These men were awake. Day was broken. In the east the sky was white.

The church-bell began to toll for Mass. From her window she could see the village. The hills opposite were black, hard as cast-iron against the whitening sky. A halo already stood over the place where the sun would mount, and a cloud high up was shot with gold. Noémi was shivering with cold. She rose and paced the chamber, but ever and anon returned to the window to look out. The white light was changing to amber, the sun was at hand.

Roger was carolling merrily, and smoke issued from the guard-chamber. The men were lighting a fire whereat to warm themselves, and perhaps do some cooking for their morning meal. In the cold meadow by the water-side, where lay a whiteness like a snow, a peasant was visible, turning the glebe with his plough fastened to the horns of a pair of oxen.

She paced her chamber faster. She could not overcome the shivering that pervaded her. The cold had entered the marrow of her bones, and with it her heart turned sick. Where was Jean? Was he in the oubliette? Had he been cast down on the body of his dying father?

Suddenly Noémi stood still. Painted on the rock opposite the window was a saffron spot of light. The sun was risen.

"It is all over!" she said, and went to the door.

There she uttered a cry—a cry of joy and release.

Along the surface of the rock ran Jean towards her. He leaped on the threshold, and she caught and drew him in with both hands.

The chill had gone from her. A rush of glowing life swept through her arteries and suffused her cheeks.

"Saved!" she gasped. "Oh, Jean, is it well?"

"I am but just in time!" he answered. "All is well. I came on—my father is behind, too tired to proceed at my pace. Oh, Noémi, Noémi—"

They held hands, they could neither speak more words. Her eyes filled with tears, and then she sobbed.

Jean was moved. "Noémi," he said, "I shall never, never forget what you have done for us."

The girl speedily recovered herself.

"I must back to Domme," she said. "My task is done. You did not say that I had surrendered myself?"

"No. I let Le Gros Guillem think that we had captured you. But it is with me as with you. I must be back to my father. There is a fellow come with me—called Heliot, and with my father is Peyrot le Fort."

"The worst—the most treacherous ruffians there are!"

"They can do no hurt. At all events, till you are restored."

"From that moment their hands are free."

Jean became grave for a moment. But his was an honest nature, not prone to mistrust, even in the midst of the lawlessness and falsehood of the times.

"Ah, bah!" said he. "I can defend myself!"

"Then let us start immediately," said Noémi. "I would that you had not to come back with me. I would your father had not been left with Peyrot le Fort."

Jean went into his father's castle. He ordered two men-at-arms to attend him. Roger and Amanieu were as well to accompany the Captain's daughter.

In less than an hour all were ready to start. A breakfast was hastily snatched, and Jean's horse, as well as that of the routier, was given water and corn.

The band of men that left Ste. Soure consisted now of Jean del' Peyra, with his two men mounted, also of Noémi, attended by three of her father's routiers.The men whom Jean had taken with him as attendants were not accustomed to riding; they could handle a pike, but had not been called to service on horseback, and this became speedily evident, for on descending a hill which was rough with chalk nodules and flints, one of them let his horse fall, and himself rolled some way down. The beast was injured and the man bruised. To Jean's annoyance he was not only detained, but obliged to leave the fellow behind. He was engaged for some minutes examining the horse's knees and satisfying himself that the brute was not in a condition to go further.

When he rejoined Noémi she said to him in a low tone—

"Let the men ride on; I have a word to say to you."

Jean slackened pace and waited till a sufficient distance separated them from their attendants. Then she said: "Treachery is intended. Heliot has been working Amanieu and Roger. Amanieu says he will do nothing; observe him now. He has thrust his hands into his belt; that means that he will neither serve Le Gros Guillem nor Del' Peyra, but let the others do as they list. As for Roger, he has pretended to agree, and he has cautioned me. He does not know particulars. Heliot would not trust him—he only sounded Roger."

"The fellow shall at once be disarmed," said Jean, and rode forward. The routier was summoned to deliver up his sword, and seeing that he could obtain no assistance from his former comrades, sullenly surrendered. He was then allowed to ride on with the rest, but with his hands bound.

In the meanwhile the other routier had been spending the remainder of the night by the charcoal-burner's pile. He found the peasant churlish and indisposed for conversation, wary, and watchful of all his movements. Now and again, when the collier was engaged on his heap, Peyrot stole into the hut to look at the sleeping Seigneur, but immediately was followed by the burner with his pronged fork.

"Why do you always run after me?" he asked churlishly.

"Because I know that such as you purpose no good."

In the morning the old Seigneur awoke, and came forth. He said nothing, but as he looked at the collier, who was eating brown bread, the man concluded he was hungry, and readily shared his breakfast with him, but absolutely refused to break bread with the rover. Peyrot was hungry, and irritated because he was not given the opportunity of executing his intention. He would have attacked the collier but that he feared him; the man was tall, muscular, and on the alert. His black face disguised his feelings, but his eyes flashed with a saturnine light at every suspicious movement of the man-at-arms.

"They come! they come!" shouted the charcoal-burner, starting forward.

"They come!" echoed Peyrot, and at once he had his sword out, and had struck at Ogier from behind. The blow would have been fatal had not the old man worn Le Gros Guillem's jerkin lined with ring mail. In a moment Peyrot was caught by the fork of the collier, round the throat, under chin and ears, was flung backwards and pinned to the ground.

"Haro! help all! I have the wolf!" yelled the man, and from out of the scrub poured the peasants returning from the chase.

They had been so far successful that they had killed the male wolf and the cubs, but the dam had escaped them. They were exultant, excited by the hunt; they carried the beasts they had killed slung across poles.

"See here!" cried the collier. "Here is the worst wolf of all—he tried to murder the Sieur del' Peyra!"

"We will drive him into your charcoal and burn him!" cried a peasant.

"That will spoil my charcoal. He is not worth it," answered the collier.

"We will hack him to pieces!" "We will cudgel out his brains!" "We will flay him alive!" As many voices, so many opinions.

At the same time arrived the party from Le Peuch.

"Here are others! See! Another red cross! Burn—hang—brain them both! Here are other two! Kill them all—all!"

The peasants seethed and swirled round Heliot, whose hands were bound, and about Amanieu and Roger.

"My friends," said Jean del' Peyra, "you are mistaken. This is my prisoner. The others are my very good friends."

"You would not let us kill them before, and now this fellow tried to murder your father. He struck at him from behind like a coward."

"If he has done that," said Jean, "his life is forfeit. Who says he did that?"

"I do," answered the collier. "I saw him. He has been looking out for an opportunity all morning. I saved the Seigneur."

"Very well," said Jean. "Then I speak no word in his behalf. Let him be taken to the next tree and hanged."

"Hang him! hang him! who has a rope? That which fastens the old wolf will do! No—it is too short, make a band of hazel."

Then a voice shouted: "There is before you Le Gros Guillem's daughter. Why should we kill the wolf's cubs and let run Guillem's whelps?"

"Kill her! kill the whelp!" yelled the men, and crowded round Noémi.

"She is a Tarde! Hands off!" called another. "Take the men, do not touch a woman!"

Then the crowd precipitated itself on the bound routier; Amanieu and Roger drew their swords and kept the peasants at bay.

"She is a cub of Gros Guillem, I swear it!" called a man. "Kill the whole breed, or she will mother loups-garoug!" (Were-wolves.)

"Messire Jean! we have no cause against you," said an immense man, a farmer, coming up and laying hold of Jean's horse's bridle. "But we will not spare any of that Domme race. They are accursed—have they not been excommunicated by the Pope—by the Bishop? We do not spare a wolf-cub however piteously it whine, however young it be, to whatever sex it may belong; and if this be a cub of the were-wolf Guillem, shall we be squeamish? Swear to us she is not of the race, and she shall pass untouched. If not, we will kill her."

Densely packed round him, brandishing forks and clubs and axes were the men, rendered savage by oppression, and now reckless by success. None were the retainers of the Del' Peyras. Jean knew not to what master they belonged. The men roared—

"Swear she is not Guillem's daughter, or we will kill her!"

The moment was one of supreme danger.

"Noémi!" said he hastily. "Hold out thy hand!"

She obeyed, extending her fingers straight before her.

"Swear! swear!" yelled the men.

Then Jean plucked open his purse, drew out the ring she had sent by him to her father, and said, as he held it aloft—

"See all; I put it on her finger. Do you want to know who she is? Know all that she is the betrothed of Jean del' Peyra, son of the Sieur del Peuch de Ste. Soure."

A shriek—a shriek of horror and agony.

The attention of those crowding in on Noémi and Jean was diverted.

Some men had taken up Peyrot le Fort, and had rammed him with their pitchforks into the fuming pyre of the charcoal-burner, then had massed on sods and clay, and had beat it down over him with their spades.

"Ride! away! ride!" shouted Jean.


CHAPTER XXI

A DISAPPEARANCE

The old Seigneur del' Peyra was not exactly a changed man since his descent into and release from the oubliette; he was rather the man he had been of old with his dullness, inertness intensified. He spoke very little, never referred to his adventures—it might almost be thought that he had forgotten them, but that on the smallest allusion to Le Gros Guillem his eye would fire, all the muscles of his face quiver, and he would abruptly leave the society of such as spoke of the man who had so ill-treated him.

Except for the sudden agitations into which he was thrown by such allusions, he was almost torpid. He took no interest in his land, in his people, in his castle. He sat much on a stone in the sun when the sun shone, looking at the ground before him. When the cold and rainy weather set in, then he sat in the fire-corner with his eyes riveted on the flames. One thing he could not endure, and that was darkness. The coming on of night filled him with unrest. He could not abide in a room where did not burn a light. He would start from sleep during the night several times to make sure that the lamp was still burning.

At first Jean had spoken to his father relative to the incidents of his capture, and had asked him particulars about his treatment, but desisted from doing so as he saw how profoundly it affected the old man, and how slow he was of recovering his equanimity after such an attempt to extract his recollections from him. Nor could he consult him about the affairs of the Seigneurie. The old man seemed incapable of fixing his mind on any such matters. Not that his brain had ceased to act, but that it was preoccupied with one absorbing idea, from which it resented diversion.

Jean made an attempt to sound his father's thoughts, but in vain, and he satisfied himself that the only course open to him was to leave the old man alone, and to trust to the restorative forces of Nature to recover him. He had received a shock which had shaken his powers but had not destroyed them. If left alone he would in time be himself again.

There was much to occupy the mind and take up the time of Jean del' Peyra.

The winter had set in. The leaves had been shed from the trees. There had set in a week of rain, and the river Vézère had swelled to a flood red-brown in colour, sweeping away the soil rich in phosphates that overlay the chalk, and which alone sustained vegetation. If the Vézère were in flood, so also was the

Dordogne, and both rivers being impassable, the little Seigneurie of Le Peuch Ste. Soure was safe. It was divided from its foe at Domme by these swollen dykes.

But floods would subside in time, the weather would clear, and although it was not probable that Le Gros Guillem would attempt reprisals during the winter, yet it would be injudicious not to maintain watch and be prepared against an attack.

The peasant, impulsive and inconsiderate, was not to be trusted without direction, and required to be watched so as to be kept to the ungrateful task of semi-military service. He was easily stirred to acts of furious violence, and as easily allowed himself to lapse into blind security. Having taken and destroyed l'Église and beaten back the routiers on the Beune, the peasants considered that they had done all that could be required of them; they hastily reconverted their swords into the ploughshares that they had been, and dismounted their spears to employ them for their proper use as pruning-hooks. At the same time that they thus turned their implements of husbandry to peaceful ends, so did they dismantle themselves of all military ambition, and revert to the condition of the boor, whose thoughts are in the soil he turns and returns, whose produce he reaps and mows. The peasant mind is not flexible, and it is very limited in its range. It can think of but one thing at a time, and it is wholly void of that nimbleness which is acquired by association with men of many avocations and of intellectual culture. For a moment, stirred by intolerable wrongs, his passions had flared into an all-consuming flame. Now he was again the plodding ploughman, happy to handle the muckfork and the goad.

Jean found it impossible to rouse the men to understand the necessity of being ever on the alert against the foe. Gros Guillem, said they, had pillaged Ste. Soure; he had done his worst; now he would go and plunder elsewhere. He had tried conclusions with them and had been worsted; in future he would test his strength against weaker men. Allons! we have had enough of fighting—there is much to be done on the farm. Jean del' Peyra foresaw danger, and would not relax his efforts to be prepared to meet it. He established sentinels to keep watch night and day, and he marshalled the peasants and drilled them. They grumbled, and endeavoured to shirk, and he had hard matter to enforce discipline. He received tidings from Domme, and ascertained that the feet of the Captain were completely restored; and that he was about the town and citadel as usual.

He had matter to occupy him and divert his attention from Le Peuch. For some time the great stress of war between the French and the English had been in the north; there the Maid of Orleans had led to victory, and there she had been basely deserted and allowed to fall into the hands of the English. No sooner, however, had these latter burnt "the sorceress" than they turned their attention to Guyenne. There matters had not been favourable to the three Leopards. Bergerac, on the Dordogne, an important mercantile centre devoted to the French cause, and which had been long held by the English, had been freed, and had the Lilies waving from its citadel. Then suddenly the English forces from Bordeaux had appeared under the walls, and the garrison, unable to defend itself unassisted, had fled, and once more the Lilies were thrown down and the Leopards unfurled. But recently, owing to some outrage committed in the town by some of the soldiers of the castle, the whole of the inhabitants had risen in a mass, had surprised the garrison, and had butchered them to a man. Bergerac was again French. For the last time it had borne the English yoke. During three hundred years, with the exception of a few intervals, it had been under English dominion (1150-1450), many a time had French and English fought under its walls for the possession of such a strong point, which by its position commanded the course of the Dordogne. Tradition even says that in one day the town passed thrice into English and thrice into French hands.

The recovery of Bergerac by the Count of Penthièvre, the Lieutenant of the King of France in Guyenne, and the treatment of the garrison by the citizens, alarmed Le Gros Guillem. He was keenly alive to the disaffection of the town of Domme. He was in a less satisfactory position than the commandant of Bergerac. For this latter place was surrounded by strongholds of barons attached to the English cause, not on principle, but for their own interest; the nearest town up the river, Le Linde, was a bastide in English hands. The heights bristled with castles, all held by men strongly opposed to the crown of France, all ready to harass in every way the citizens who had dared to free themselves. The situation at Domme was other. Nearly in face of it was a town almost as important in population, quite as securely defended by Nature, and dominated by a castle of exceptional inexpugnability. The Governor of this place was the brother of the Bishop of Sarlat, and could not be bribed to betray his charge. From his eyrie every movement of Guillem was watched. La Roque was a stronghold with the whole county of Sarlat at its back, and thence it could be filled with men unseen from Domme, to organise a sudden attack on the enemy's position. That alone might be repelled, but that aided by treachery within the walls might succeed.

Consequently Guillem was engaged in filling his ranks and accumulating material of war. Desire as he might, and did, to chastise those at Ste. Soure, he could not do so at the moment.

Never did he ride by La Roque without casting on it a covetous gaze. It was the key to the whole of the Black Périgord—the county of Sarlat.

Jean del' Peyra's mind reverted often to Noémi. He had not seen her since that incident of the ring. Then, attended by Amanieu and Roger, she had ridden away at full gallop and had escaped. At the same time he had succeeded in cutting the bands that held the arms of Heliot, and had suffered him to ride away as well. Jean was naturally adverse to deeds of bloodshed; and though the fellow justly merited death, he had no desire that the peasantry should constitute themselves at once accusers, judges, and executioners. Jean thought repeatedly of that strange scene—his engagement by ring to Noémi, forced on him to save her from the violence of the angry peasants—the only means available to him at the moment for evading the question as to her parentage.

But though he had quickly proclaimed her to be his affianced bride, he did not seriously purpose to make her his. Though he loved her, though his heart eagerly recognised her generosity of feeling, the real goodness that was in her, he could not forget to what stock she belonged. It would not be possible for him to consider her as one who would be his—when he was at deadly enmity with the father. It would not be decent, natural, to take to his side the child of the ruffian who had treated his own father in a manner of refined barbarity. It was known throughout the country what Guillem had done—and the whole country would point the finger of scorn at him if he so condoned the outrage as to marry the daughter of the perpetrator of it. But, more than that, he was certain to be engaged in hand-to-hand fight with Guillem. He did not for a moment doubt that this man would seize the first opportunity of attacking and probably of overwhelming him with numbers. When next they met the meeting would be final, and fatal to one or the other. Either he or Le Gros Guillem would issue from the struggle with his hands wet with the blood of the other. It mattered not which turn matters took, what the result was— either precluded union with Noémi.

He would have liked to have seen her, to have parted from her with words of gratitude for what she had done for him and his father. He would have liked to come to an understanding with her. She was not a child, surely she did not hold those words spoken by him, that ring put on her finger, as binding them together?

He was thinking over this, scheming how he could meet her, when one of his men came to him and said—

"Monsieur Jean, have you seen your father?"

"When? Just now?"

"Yes," said the man, "recently."

"No, Antoine, not for several hours."

"Nor has anyone else."

"Not seen my father?"

"No, Monsieur Jean, we have been looking for him in every direction, and cannot find him."

"He is in the castle."

"No, Monsieur Jean, there he is not."

"He is in the field."

"No, Monsieur Jean, he is nowhere."

"That is not possible."

"He is nowhere that we can find, and no one has seen him leave—no one knows whether he has been carried off again, and if so, how, when, or by whom?"

It was so—Ogier del' Peyra had vanished, not leaving a trace behind him.


CHAPTER XXII

THE CASTELLAN

Le Gros Guillemwas pacing the stone-vaulted hall of the Castle of Domme. It was a hall that ran the whole depth of the castle, from one face to the other, and was lighted solely by large windows to the north, commanding the valley of the Dordogne. The room was vaulted, not ribbed; cradled with white stone, the walls were of stone, and the hall was paved with stone—all of one whiteness. No tapestry covered the naked sides, nor carpets clothed the floors, only some panelling of oak to man's height took off some of the chill of the walls, and straw was littered on the floor. Of ornament there was none in the hall, unless weapons and defensive armour might be so regarded. Even antlers and boars' heads were absent. The occupants of the castle had other amusements than the chase.

"I must have thirty men more," said the Captain. "Let Heliot ride into the Bretenoux country; he will get them there; and let that sulky Amanieu, who is neither one of us nor against us, go to Gramat, on the bald and barren Causse, where nothing grows save lank and hungry men, there is always a supply of daredevils to be had for the asking. Offer what you will—we must make an attempt on Bergerac—and have the looting of its fat merchants' houses. We will make a raid into Sarlat and put the oily canons into the olive-press. There is plenty to be had for the taking. I want men. I must have more men. I dare not leave Domme without a thumb on it to hold it down; and there is that accursed eye of La Roque watching unwinkingly. Fine times are coming. I hear that the English are sending an army under the great Talbot. Let us do something—pick over the vineyard before he comes or the Englishmen will have the biggest bunches."

One of the attendants came up to the Captain and informed him that there was an old man desired to speak with him.

"What does he want? Where does he come from? I want no old men. The young are those who can serve me. I have not here an almshouse for bedemen, but a training school for soldiers."

"He will not say what he wants—except only that he comes on matters of extreme importance."

"Importance! importance!" repeated Le Gros Guillem irritably. "Importance to him and not to me. What is he? a farmer? Some of my boys have lifted an ox or carried off a daughter. I will not see him."

"Captain, he comes from La Roque."

"Then I will have nothing to do with him. I have no dealings with the people of La Roque. Run your pikes into his calves and make him skip down the hill."

The attendant retired but returned shortly with a slip of paper, which he put into the Captain's hand. Guillem would have thrust it aside. "A scribbling petitioner—worst of all! Does he look as if he had money? Can he be made to pay? If so we will put him in the mortar and pound him."

With careless indifference Guillem opened the paper and read the lines—

Messire le Gros,—If you want a lodging in La Roque now is your opportunity. From one who has charge of the keys.

"Eh! eh!" exclaimed the Captain, flushing over his bald head, and his long fingers crushed the paper in excitement. "What! a chance of that? Show him in—and you, guard, stand at a distance at the door."

In another moment an old man with short-cut grey hair was introduced. He walked with the aid of a stick, and kept his eyes on the ground. He was habited in a shabby dark suit, out at elbows, somewhat clerical in cut, and he was shaved like a priest. His face was singularly mottled, in places yellow with sunburn, elsewhere white. He had bushy eyebrows that contrasted singularly with his close-clipped head and his smooth jaws.

"So!" said Guillem, striding up to him, "you have the keys—and who are you?"

"Messire Captain, I am your very humble servant."

"To the point! What are you at La Roque, and what do you want with me?"

"Messire, I am now caretaker of the fortress in the cliff. I hold the keys and am responsible for its custody."

"And what brings you here?"

"Messire, I am willing to let you in."

"Ah! On what terms?"

"Messire—I trust to your generosity."

"That is not a usual mode of doing business. Why do you come to me? Why betray your trust? There is a reason—is it money? I will pay. What do you demand?"

"I ask no money."

"Then in Heaven's name what do you want?"

"Revenge!" answered the old man, and bowed his head lower over his staff.

"Revenge! Hah! I can understand that. Revenge on someone in La Roque?"

"On someone who is not there now, but who will be there on the night that I admit you."

"And you ask me to revenge your wrong."

"I will do that for myself, Messire—only I can do nothing now. I am prepared to admit you within the walls of the town. I can do better than that—I will give you access to the castle—the town without the castle is nothing. The castle in itself is nothing. But the castle commands the town."

"Hah! let us in, within the walls of La Roque, and we will soon have the castle."

"You think that, Messire? You are mistaken. The castle is victualled for three months. There is a well in it that never runs dry. There is a garrison under the Sieur François de Bonaldi, brother of the Bishop. If you took the town with my help, it would be cracking the nut and not getting the kernel. From the castle they could rain down rocks on you, and if you attempted to hold the town they would dislodge you, though it might ruin the houses. No—the town without the castle is an eyeball without the iris. Take the castle and the town is yours."

"You may be right," said Le Gros Guillem, after a pause.

"I am positive I am right," said the old man, looking up and dropping his eyes again.

"What, then, do you propose?"

"On a night—let us say to-morrow before midnight, I will admit you and five men—"

"Why not more?"

"Harken. Messire, I have thought the plan out."

"Go on!—I am impatient to hear."

"It is you, Messire le Gros, who have interrupted me."

"Go on with your plan! If I do not approve, I will none of it. I am not going to run into a trap."

"A trap! Oh, Messire, how can you think of that?"

"Tell me your plan at once."

"It is this, Messire. I will let you in through the postern gate on the upper—the Vitrac—Sarlat Road, you and five men—no more. As many as you will need can be admitted later; they shall remain without till the castle is in your hands, and then two of your men who will tarry by the gate will unbar to them and let them all enter. But consider, Messire, it will not do to allow access to more than five at the outset— there are sentinels on the walls. I have no understanding with them, and they might see and give the alarm. If the alarm were given before you had obtained possession of the castle, then the whole expedition would be in vain. If you hold the castle you have the heart of La Roque Gageac in your hands."

"And you will admit us into the fortress?"

"I will admit you and three men."

"It is not enough."

"It suffices. There are but six men in the castle—and no guard is kept at night, for none is needed, as you will see when you get there. That on the town walls suffices; one of these men is in agreement with me. Him you must pay, but not me. I shall be well indemnified if I get my revenge."

"So then—you will first open the gate to me and five men. Then, two are to be left in charge of the gate, I and three others are next to be given admittance to the castle, where we are to overpower the garrison. You say there are but six men. That is very few."

"Messire, the Bishop says he can afford no more, and his brother, the Sieur François, has written to urge him to supply him with more, but he says that his treasury is exhausted and his land impoverished, and that there are no more men to be got. Besides, what they reckon on is for the whole garrison of the town to fly to the castle should the walls of the town fall into the enemy's power. It has never entered into their heads that the citadel should be first grasped, and the citadel commands all—it commands the town, it commands the road to Sarlat, it commands the whole country."

"And the Bishop says there is nothing to be got—no money?"

"So he says; that is the reason he gives. He told the Sieur François to do his best with the handful he has; he was unable to assist further."

"We will speedily prove if his words be true. We shall soon make him beat his head to think that he was so parsimonious that he had scruples about melting up his church plate. That only is an exhausted land which yields naught when it has passed through my sieve." Guillem halted in his walk, laid one hand on the shoulder of the old man, and said, in a tone in which was some suspicion, "So you will turn traitor, betray a trust for nothing!"

"Pardon, Messire; I said that I did it to satisfy my revenge."

"By the Holy Caul of Cahors!"[5] laughed Le Gros Guillem, "revenge is sweet, especially to the old. When the kisses of women and the clink of spurs and the fingering of gold no longer charm, revenge is still palatable. What makes you so lust for vengeance, old man?"

[5] La Sainte Coiffe—a caul in which it was fabled that the infant Christ was born—was one of the choice relics preserved at Cahors. It fell into the hands of the Huguenots at the memorable capture of Cahors by Henry of Navarre, but was recovered. It happily disappeared at the Revolution.

"Ah, Messire! what do the small troubles of a nobody like me concern you?"

Guillem let go his hold and recommenced his pacing: "The Holy Caul to my aid! but I, too, have my grievance, and my mouth waters for the same dainty as does yours. Let me but be established at La Roque, and they may expect me at Le Peuch."

"Who is at Le Peuch, Messire?"

"Old man, one who has injured my honour; one to whom I will show no mercy if I but get him in my grip. From La Roque I can command all the Sarladais, and I can swoop down at my leisure on Le Peuch. I shall get gold at Sarlat and blood at Le Peuch. By Heaven, I do not know which will best please me!"

"You accept my offer, Messire le Gros?"

"Aye—to-morrow, at an hour to midnight. Are you an ecclesiastic?"

"No, Messire."

"You have a clerical aspect; but I suppose all who serve the Bishop assume something of that. Very well. I shall be there—I and my men. Will you eat? Will you drink?"

"Thank you, Messire. I have not come from far—only across the water. The ferryman put me over. I made some excuse that I had a married daughter to visit, and none suspect evil; but I must make speed and return before mistrust breeds. Mistrust will spoil all, Messire."

"Very well. Go! So we meet to-morrow. If you fail—if you prove false, old man—terrible will be your lot."

"I shall not fail. Fear not. I shall not eat, I shall not sleep; I shall count the hours till you come."

Le Gros Guillem mused a moment. Then he said: "What shall be the sign by which you will know we are there—at the gate?"

"You will come," answered the old man, "to the little postern at the Sarlat gate. It lays on the right—twenty strides up the slope; you pass by a vineyard to it. I will tarry there till I hear you scratch like a cat."

"Very well—and the word?"

"The word—for a merry jest—as you said it, Le Peuch."

"Le Peuch—so be it," said the Captain. "Further—the main body of men will be posted outside, and they are not to be admitted till the castle is ours. How shall I communicate with them?"

"Nothing is easier," replied the castellan. "When Messire is above, and has got the men of the garrison bound, let him ring the alarm-bell. It is in the tower of the castle gate, and at once your men below will admit their fellows, and the townsfolk will awake to discover themselves betrayed, and in the hands of the illustrious and very generous Captain Guillem."

"It is good!" said the routier."You have thought this plan well out, old man."

"Oh, I have thought it well out. I have been long about it. I took much consideration before all was fitted together. So—there—all is agreed. I wish you well till we meet."

The castellan made for the door, but before he reached it, he rested on his staff, and burst into a convulsive fit of laughter.

"What is that?" asked the Captain, coming towards him. "What makes you laugh?"

"Excuse me, Messire. I am old, and my nerves are shaken. I have had much to agitate them—and these convulsive fits come on me—when I think I am on the eve of a great pleasure—and it will be a great pleasure," he turned and bowed, and made a salutation with his cap, and with extended hands—"ah! Messire a great pleasure, to open the gate, and let you in!" He bowed profoundly, and went out backwards laughing and saluting.

CHAPTER XXIII

IN THE HAIL

Le Gros Guillem was jubilant. He kept his secret. Not to one of his men—not even to his lieutenant did he confide his purpose of surprising the castle and town of La Roque Gageac, for he well knew that no secret is safe when once it has slipped over the lips.

He was in excellent spirits, in buoyant, boisterous humour. He laughed and joked with his men, and Guillem was too grim a man to be often given to jest. He bade his men look to their arms, and he detailed those who were to follow him on an expedition. Whither he was going he did not say—but with him that was usual—he let no breath of rumour escape as to his destination whenever he made a raid, and on this account he was almost always successful; he came down like a bolt out of the sky on some spot, totally unprepared to resist him, and none could betray his scheme, and prepare those fallen upon, for none knew his destination till he started.

"Heliot!" called Guillem, suddenly arresting himself as he was drawing a long sword from the scabbard to examine if it were free of rust. "Did you observe that old man who was here last evening?"

"I saw him come in, Captain."

"But—there is something in his face familiar to me—I fancy I have seen him before—and yet—I am not sure."

"He said that he came from Gageac and had relatives in this town."

"That may be it. To be sure—he told me, a married daughter—I have seen him here at some fair, may be. It will not out of my head, I have seen him—and cannot say where. He looks like a broken priest."

"As he walked he was bowed, and I could not see his face, Captain," answered Heliot.

"It matters not. Is there any moon to-night, Heliot?"

"There is a new moon, Captain; you can see her in the sky, she does not set till early morning, just before daybreak. But we shall see little of her tonight; there are thick clouds coming up against the wind—piled up as though full of thunder."

"So much the better. Heliot, I will tell you now what is to be done—we must cross the Dordogne." More than that he would not say.

The city of Sarlat lies at a distance of several miles from the river, and is accessible by two valleys, one of which opens on to the Dordogne under the rock of Vitrac, a sheer limestone cliff, the top of which is occupied by a village and castle, the foot bathed by the river, and the defile up which the road runs commanded not only by the castle of Vitrac, but by another, a tower on the further side, and these two were designed to completely bar the way to the town. The other way is more tortuous, and was also defended both by the great castle and rock of Beynac and also by a low hill in the midst of the open valley that was likewise fortified. The situation may be best understood if we imagine a great triangular plateau with Sarlat at the apex and the Dordogne flowing at the base; midway on that base stands La Roque.

With the river thus watched and every road guarded jealously, it was important for Le Gros Guillem to cross in the dark, unperceived, lest a warning should be sent to La Roque, and the garrison be set on the alert so that the castellan would be unable to fulfil his engagement.

As the evening closed in the clouds that had been noticed by Heliot covered the whole heavens. There was no wind below; at the same time one must have been blowing aloft, for the vapours parted and disclosed the moon and then drifted over its face again, and through them it peered dimly, like an eye with cataract over it, or else became totally obscured.

The men detailed for the expedition were assembled in the courtyard of the castle. They were not mounted—horses were unnecessary and inconvenient. The tramp might be heard and cause alarm. The routiers remained in their ranks motionless till the word was given, and then silently they defiled out of the castle, through the street of Domme, and the town portcullis was raised to allow them to pass forth.

Le Gros Guillem had boats on the river at his command. And the passage of the Dordogne was effected in the darkness successfully without attention being attracted on the opposite bank. The companions issued from the boats and drew up on the bank till the Captain gave the command to march, when they proceeded down the right bank of the river without speaking and without making any noise. Owing to the rainfall the way was muddy and the mud prevented their tramp from being audible. Shortly before the hour named by the castellan the entire party was near the Sarlat gate, concealed behind vineyard walls and bushes.

The town that was menaced seemed to be buried in slumber and security. The only light discernible was the faint glow through the church window of S. Donat, where the sanctuary lamp burned. There was not even a light in the castle—which in the general darkness was indiscernible—only the mighty cliff into which it was built stood high overhead like a gigantic wave ready to fall and bury everything beneath it. The Captain picked out the men he had fixed on to accompany him and gave his instructions to the others in a whisper. As soon as the alarm-bell sounded in the castle they were to draw rapidly to the gate. Their comrades within would open, "and," said Guillem, "the town is yours—to do as you please therein.' Then he advanced cautiously with his five men to the postern at the side and not to the main gate. This postern was small, it would admit but one man at a time.

On reaching it Guillem scratched with the point of his sword, and the signal was answered at once—cautiously the door was unbarred and unlocked and the castellan appeared in it. The clouds had momentarily parted and the new moon gleamed forth and was reflected by the river. Guillem could perceive that this was the same man who had visited him at Domme.

"The word?"

"Le Peuch."

"It is well, Le Peuch. How many?" he asked under his breath.

"Myself and five," answered Guillem.

"It is well—let two men remain here. The others follow me." He led the way up a steep stair of stone steps, past houses built into the rock, past the little church, one wall of which was the rock itself, and the roadway lay almost level with the eave. There was a clock in the tower, it throbbed like the pulse of a living being—the pulse of the whole town, but it beat evenly, as if the town was without fear.

The road lay beneath some houses; for, in order to penetrate from one portion of the town to another, to reach from one ledge of rock with the buildings occupying it where every foot of ground was precious, the path was conducted beneath chambers, in which, overhead, the citizens were peacefully sleeping unsuspicious of what was proceeding below.

In another moment the platform had been reached below the sheer cliff that rose without so much as a shelf on which a shrub could root itself, even of a cranny in which a pink or harebell might cling.

All was now so dark that Guillem could not see his guide or his men.

Not a sound had been heard in the town—and here there was nothing audible save a cat that was mewing. It had been shut out of a house and feared that a storm was coming on. The time was winter, the little creature was cold, and it craved for the warmth and the dryness of the kitchen hearth. The foolish cat came up to Le Gros Guillem and rubbed herself against his legs and pleaded for attention. Irritated at her persistence and cries, the Captain dealt her a kick which sent her flying and squealing. Then he regretted that he had done this, lest her shrill cry should reach the mistress and induce her to open the door and show a light.

But no token followed and showed that the cat had been heard. Again the creature came near, mewing. The darkness was so dense that nothing could be seen, not even the rock in front, only the buildings round loomed black against the sky that was but a shade lighter than the rock.

Then hail rushed down, hissing, leaping, and with the hail a flash of lightning revealing the blank wall of rock in front and the floor over which the hailstones ran and spun.

"Where is the stair?" asked Le Gros Guillem of the castellan, who kept at his side.

"Stair—what stair?"

"The way by which we are to mount into the castle?"

The old man chuckled.

"Wait a while," said he in a whisper. "When next the lightning flashes look ahead of you—a little to the right, and you will see a cobweb path up the face of the rock."

"Lead us to the path—cobweb or not we will mount it. We are accustomed to that, and this is tedious—tarrying here. Curse that cat! Here she is again!"

"Ah, Messire—you do not comprehend. Have you never been in La Roque?"

"I? Never! Do you suppose they would suffer me within the walls?"

"Then, Messire, you cannot understand how it is that of the garrison none are awake, how it comes that there is no need for watchfulness. Wait a while, the lightning—there—did you see?"

The old man pointed in the direction of the stair. The construction of this path of ascent has been already described. It consisted of a ladder of pegs driven into the rock, each peg sustained by a wedge underneath it. Nothing was easier than by a blow to loosen the wedge and to throw the steps down, and when down no passage could be effected to or from the castle along the face of the rock.

"Did you observe?" asked the old man.

"I observed nothing save a stair."

"Look at the base of the stair. Ah! the hail! how it whitens the ground, how it lights up the landscape. One can see a little now, and presently, if you will have patience, Messire, I will explain it all."

"I want no explanation, I want to mount the stair and enter the castle."

"You cannot mount the stair. It is not possible. There—another flash—now do you see? All the lower portion is removed, so that, till put together again in the morning, no one can ascend. Moreover, there aloft is a landing place, and between that landing place and the gate there is a gap—and over that a draw-plank is lowered. Now, at night, all the lowest rungs of the stair are taken away and above the plank is lifted. There is no possibility of anyone mounting by that means."

"Then, in the devil's name, why have you brought us here? I tell you, old man, I will drive my poignard down your throat if you have dared to deceive me."

"I deceive you! Oh, Messire! There is a second way of entering the castle."

"And that is—?"

"See!"

Again the lightning flickered, and now the clouds parting allowed the moon to flash over the whitened earth and show the great wall of chalk rock in front mounting into the sky and white as the ghostly clouds touched by moonlight that moved above it. The freebooter saw something hanging down the face of the cliff. It was a rope, and at the end was a bar of wood some two feet long which it held in a horizontal position by a knot in the middle.

"My good friend, whom you will have to reward, is above at the windlass. You can mount, Messire. I have but to shake the cord and put my fingers into my mouth and hoot as an owl and he will begin to wind up. It is by this means that provisions are carried up, and by this one can go up or down when the passage of the stair is cut off. Will you please to mount first—or shall I, most honoured Captain?" The castellan took off his hat and bowed.

Le Gros Guillem looked up a sheer height of a hundred feet; in the uncertain light it appeared as though this cord was let down out of the sky. He was a man who rarely knew fear—in the heat of conflict he never knew it at all. He was dauntless in every daring feat; but this was a venture sufficient to make even him hesitate. He knew not who was the man at the capstan above. He was not sure that the rope would endure his weight.

"Oh," said the castellan, "if you are afraid to trust yourself to this cord, you must e'en return by the way you came. I thought other of Le Gros Guillem, of the famous Captain. I did not think he would quail as a girl from such a trifle as this. I will ascend first, and then you may pluck up heart to follow an old man."

The castellan went to the rope and shook it twice, then imitated the scream of an owl, and instantly planted himself on the pole and held the cord with both hands. He began at once to ascend.

The sky cleared of thunder-cloud and the wan new moon illumined the scene. The rock was white, and against it mounted a dark figure with a darker shadow. The windlass moved noiselessly; Le Gros Guillem and his men below heard no sound. The dark figure slid up the rock and became smaller, ever smaller, and then disappeared. In the uncertain light, at the great elevation they could not see, but supposed the castellan had passed through a window into the castle.

Then rapidly down came rope and pole, and the latter hung swaying at a couple of feet above the hail-strewn platform.

"In the devil's name, I will try it!" said Guillem, and committec himself to the bar. He grasped the rope and hooted. At the same moment the cat leaped and lighted on his shoulder. He would have thrust it off, but could not. The rope had tightened, was straining, and he was carried upwards off his feet.

CHAPTER XXIV

THE FOURTH TIME

The rock of Gageac somewhat overhung, so that as Le Gros Guillem ascended he swung clear in space. Only occasionally was there a projection against which he could apply his foot, but he avoided doing this lest he should set the cord in oscillation.

The rope was so stout and the piece of wood on which he was seated so strong, that the momentary qualm that had come over his heart left it, and he felt naught save impatience to reach the castle and creep in at the window. Then his comrades would be drawn up and all four would fall on the sleeping garrison, kill every man, ring the tocsin, and the place would be in his possession, the houses given up to pillage and the inhabitants to outrage and murder. To win La Roque—a place that through the Hundred Years' War had not been taken, that for three centuries had defied the English—would indeed be an achievement, and one for which he could obtain any terms he liked to ask from the Earl of Shrewsbury on his arrival in Guyenne.

The clouds were dispersing, Guillem looked up, the floor of Heaven was as it were spilt over with curds; he looked down, every platform, roof, garden, was white with hail. On the horizon lightning was still fluttering. He had heard no thunder when below—he heard none now.

The Dordogne flowed black through a white world. It did not reflect the sky to one rising so high in the air above it; it was black as Acheron and seemed to have lost all flow—to be stilled in its course.

The moon was still shining on the wall of rock, Guillem's shadow passed with him, as substantial apparently as himself, undergoing strange, monkey-like contortions against the rocky inequalities. A curse on that cat! It was wailing in his ear. He turned his chin to endeavour to force the brute from his shoulder. The cat clung with its thorn-like claws that pierced his jerkin. He disengaged a hand, and laid hold of the cat, but it bit and tore at his hand, it drove its claws into his neck, and he could not shake it off without tearing away ribbons of his flesh as well.

His efforts to rid himself of the cat set the cord spinning, and the stick revolved, with him on it, and then spun back again; it began to swing, and in swinging jammed him against the rock.

He must make up his mind to endure the cat. It was but for a minute or two longer, and then he would be free, and would grasp the accursed brute and fling it down on to the houses beneath. A cat has nine lives. A cat will always fall on his feet. This puss must have more than nine lives if it escaped being dashed to pieces by such a fall.

All was hushed below.

Guillem, looking down, could see the black spots that he knew represented his three men who were to follow him.

Something brushed his face—it was a sprig of juniper—he knew it by the scent; and now he saw that he had reached that point where rock and wall were blended, the rock running up into ragged points, the gaps filled in with masonry, and finally courses of ashlar lying evenly above the rock.

He was nearing the window. In another minute he would be inside. He could hear the creak of the windlass. His progress upwards seemed to him to be extraordinarily slow. One line of wallstone, then another, then a third, then a halt.

He expected to be able to grasp the threshold of the window and to assist those within in drawing him through. But the window sill was some feet above his head; it was beyond his reach.

Why had those working the capstan ceased to turn the levers? Were they exhausted? Had they galled their hands? Half a dozen turns and he would be aloft.

At that moment, one of those inexplicable, unreasonable sensations that do occasionally seize the imagination swept over the mind of Guillem. Looking at the limestone before him, he all at once thought it resembled the flesh of old Ogier del' Peyra's face as he was lowered into the oubliette, with the light from the dungeon door sitting on it. There was absolutely no similarity save that the rock was grey, and that it was illumined by the new moon with some such a colourless cadaverous light as that which had lighted the face of the man sentenced to a living tomb.

Le Gros Guillem shook his head and closed his eyes to free himself from the impression.

Immediately the cat, driving its claws into his neck under the right ear, sprang on his head, ran up the rope and leaped in at the window above.

It was perhaps due to the fact that those working the capstan were frightened by the apparition of the beast; but suddenly the rope was run out and Guillem dropped through space, to be brought up by a jerk as those above mastered the spokes and arrested the flight of the rope.

As the falling man was stopped in his descent, the strands of the cord were strained and some snapped. The jerk would have thrown him from his seat had he not grappled the rope with desperation. He had not, however, dropped very far, and now to his great satisfaction he felt that the men above were again turning the levers, and that he was again being steadily hauled upwards. When aloft he would chastise them sharply for their scare about a cat, risking thereby his valuable life.

Again the juniper bush brushed his face, it was as an elfin hand which was thrust forth out of the rock to lay hold of him, or at least to warn him against further progress. Not a plant had been passed springing out of the sheer cliff. This juniper grew at the summit of the rock, and at its junction with the masonry of the castle.

Much time had elapsed, surely more than an hour, since he had passed through the postern gate. His men, concealed in the vineyards, must be impatient for the signal to enter the town and plunder it.

Then he heard a harsh, jarring sound like an angry growl, followed by the strokes of a bell. One—two—three—he reckoned till twelve. It was midnight.

Again he was ascending past the courses of ashlar, and again he was brought to a halt at some distance below the window.

Then, from above, through the window a face protruded that looked down on him. The moon was on the face; it was the colour of the grey rock; it was blotched like the rock, it was furrowed with age like the rock. Unlike the rock, two eyes gleamed out of it, with the moon glinting in them.

"Gros Guillem!" said the man who peered on the freebooter from above.

"Draw me up!" gasped the Captain, "or by—"

"Do you threaten—you—situated as you are?"

"I pray you give the windlass another turn."

"Ah, you pray now, Gros Guillem!"

The Captain looked above his head at the face that overhung him. There was in it something that sent the blood back to his heart. There was in it that likeness to a someone, uncertain, recalled but unidentified, that came out now with terrible distinctness, and insisted on his straining his powers for recognition.

"Gros Guillem! do you remember me? This is our final meeting—the fourth and the last!"

At that moment the tocsin pealed forth its summons from the tower. This tower, planted under a concave opening in the rock, sent out the ring of the alarm-bell multiplied thirtyfold below; it flung it forth in volumes, it sent it up and down the Dordogne valley—across it—over the level land, far, far away, wave on wave of sound through the still night.

At the first note it was as though a magic wand had touched every house in La Roque. Each window was illumined. Every door was opened, and forth burst men with torches, all fully armed.

In a moment the three companions of the Captain on the platform and the two by the postern were surrounded, disarmed, bound or cut down. In a moment, also, from orchards, vineyards, from out of barns, from behind hedgerows, rose a multitude of men, peasants, fishermen, soldiers of the Bishop, serving-men, all with what weapons they could most readily handle, and closed in on the men of Guillem who had come forward at the note of the bell with purpose to enter by the postern. Then ensued on all sides a wild hubbub of cries, shrieks, shouts of triumph, curses, prayers for mercy.

Le Gros Guillem, hanging in mid-air, heard the uproar, saw the upward glow of light, and knew that he and his had been drawn into a cleverly contrived trap, and that he was lost irretrievably. He writhed, he turned, he looked above—there he saw but the face of Ogier remorseless as fate. He looked below—there he saw his men, making desperate battle for life, and falling one by one. He could not distinguish each individual, but he saw knots of men forming whence issued cries and the clash of steel, then the knot broke up and its members dispersed seeking other clusters which they swelled, and whence issued the same cries and din of strife.

Presently a great flare of fire rose from below and illumined the whole rock of Gageac. A torch had been applied to a bonfire of faggots ready stacked on the platform. By that glare those below saw the suspended Captain, and uttered a roar of hate and savage delight. In Guillem's ears was a singing, and the growl of voices came in throbs like waves beating on his brain.

From those below rose cries of, "Cut the rope! Cast him down! We will receive him on our pikes. He shall fall into the fire!"

Slowly the cable was let out, and Guillem felt himself descending. He was glad that it was so. He desired to be in the midst of men, though these were his enemies; for he had his sword at his side and he would die fighting, wounding others, killing those who sought his life. So to perish were a death befitting a soldier—this such a death as he would hail. He put his hand to his sword and grasped the hilt. His blood that had curdled in his arteries began to pulsate, the film that had formed over his eyes was dissipated, and a flash of eager anticipation came into them.

But again the rope ceased to be let out. He was suspended just half-way between the castle and the platform below, in full view of the townsmen who had gathered there, standing at a sufficient distance not to be struck by his falling body; he was in view also of the little garrison of the castle who had clambered to the battlements and were looking over at him.

Then he heard a hammering, and saw below men employed driving the pegs into the sockets in the rock, and fastening the wedges that held them firm. No sooner was the full connection made than up the stair ran men and even women, and boys who had scrambled out of bed, and these stood in a line against the rock up the lengthy ladder-stair gazing at the suspended man. Then also from above the draw-bridge was lowered, and the men-at-arms who had been in the castle ran out of the gate and ran down the stair to have a better sight thence of the swinging, helpless man than they could from the battlements.

A terrible spectacle it was that they witnessed—such a one as could not be looked on by Christian people unmoved save in such an evil age as that, when men were rendered ferocious as wild Indians and callous to the sufferings of their brethren; a spectacle such as could not be looked on without pity save in such a place as that where all had suffered in some degree from the exactions or the barbarities of this wretched man. The flames danced and curled as if they also frolicked at the sight of the agony of the man who had so often fed them with hard-won harvests of the peasantry, and the humble goods of the cottager too worthless to be carried away.

In the glare of the leaping bonfire Le Gros Guillem was distinctly visible, looking like a monstrous yellow spider at the end of his line. He thrust out now one long leg, then another, next he extended his lengthy arms each armed with lean and bony fingers. He endeavoured to scramble into a standing position upon his bar, but failed—one side would descend before the other, and he nearly fell in attempting this impossible feat. He gripped the rope with hands and knees and endeavoured to swarm up it, but the cable was rendered slippery by its passage over a roller in the window.

Rage was in his heart, rage at being there a sight to men, women, and children, without power of spreading destruction about him before he died.

Then he swung himself laterally, hoping to be able to reach a projection of rock whence possibly he might creep up or down, or even laterally from jutting point to point, holding by his fingers till he attained the stair. As he came swinging like a pendulum he was carried close to the stairway, and those upon it held their breath and drew back against the rock, thinking he would make a leap in attempt to light on the steps. Were he to do this, then to arrest himself from falling backwards, with his long fingers he would inevitably clutch at them, and so precipitate them along with himself below.

Those persons standing on that portion of the steps within range sidled upwards or else downwards, to be out of the risk of such a danger. They could see in the upward flash of the firelight the sparkle in his great eyes as he glared at the steps, calculating his distance, making resolve to leap, and his heart failing him or his judgment assuring him that to do so were certainly fatal.

A tinkle of a little bell. The priest of S. Donat had hastily donned his surplice, and run and taken the Holy Sacrament, and was coming—he alone with a thought of mercy for the agonised, to obtain for him release, or to administer consolation in death. Before him went a boy with a lantern, ringing the bell.

Then a loud voice from below cried: "Cut the cable!" And then: "It is I—Francis Bonaldi—I, the governor, say it. Enough! Cut the cable!"

A gasp from all that multitude.

The cord had been chopped through before the priest arrived.


CHAPTER XXV

A HELEBORE WREATH

The destruction of Le Gros Guillem's body of men at La Roque Gageac was the prelude to the surrender of the citadel of Domme. The small garrison left in charge of that stronghold was panic-stricken when it heard the tidings from La Roque. The whole country was in arms. The citizens had marshalled in the square, and the soldiers, deserting the town, had taken refuge in the castle. Without head, without prospect of relief, hemmed in by the Bishop's troops that arrived from Sarlat and La Roque on one side, menaced from Beynac, where was a royal garrison, on another, and from Fénelon on a third, where the baron was loyal to the French crown as well as a personal enemy of Guillem, the remnant of the Company that had acknowledged Guillem as Captain was fain to capitulate; and the confederate troops under the governor of La Roque were content to accord terms, knowing the danger of driving these freebooters to desperation.

They were suffered to march forth with their arms. They retreated up the Dordogne to Autoire, an impregnable stronghold, at that time in the power of a Chief of Companies, who they knew would welcome them, and afford them fresh opportunities of ravage and of gaining spoil.

The history of France presents but one period of greater horror than that of the Free Companies—namely, the epoch of the wars of religion. But practically these latter wars were the outcome of the former. For three hundred years the barons and the great seigneurs of Aquitaine had been free to act in accordance with their passions, uncontrolled by any hand. They had made war against each other on no provocation; they had made the cities and commercial towns their common prey. The only possible way in which a community of peaceful citizens or of villagers could struggle on was by contracting patis or compacts with the barons, whereby they undertook to pay them an annual sum, and on this agreement were freed from vexation by his armed men. The younger sons of the barons, and bastards, collected about them the scum of society, runaway serfs, escaped felons, adventurers from Spain, from Brabant, from Italy, but chiefly Gascons, drilled them, armed them, maintained them in strict discipline, captured such castles as seemed to them most advisable centres as dominating fertile districts, or else constructed others wherever was a rock that lent itself to defence; and thence they carried their arms in all directions. They came in torrents down from the Causses and the Cevennes upon Languedoc. They ravaged Auvergne, they carried their incursions into Berry and the Limousin. The king of France, the estates of the several provinces, were powerless to rid the country of them. Again and again vast sums of money were collected and poured into their bottomless purses, and the Companions promised on receipt of these sums to surrender their castles and quit the country. But very generally they only half-fulfilled their undertaking. They yielded up a fortress or two; they drifted off over the Pyrenees into Spain, or over the Alps into Italy, and not finding there the spoil they wanted, or meeting there with reverses, they turned their faces again toward France and reoccupied their old nests or constructed fresh ones, and all the old evils returned in aggravated form.

The meciæval historian Villani, who died in 1363, gives an account of the formation of one of these terrible bands, which may serve as an example of the constitution of all. He says that in 1353 a knight of St. John of Jerusalem, wearied of his order and its discipline, renounced his vows and formed a Company of Free Companions in the marches of Ancona.

"Brother Moriale called together by letter and message a great number of soldiers out of employ. He bade them come to him, and promised to defray their expenses and to pay them for their services. This succeeded admirably; he gathered about him fifteen hundred bassinets and more than two thousand comrades, all men greedy to live at the cost of others." Very speedily this Company began its ravages. "They rode about the country and pillaged on all sides. They attacked Feltramo, took it by storm and killed five hundred men. As the country round was rich they remained in Feltramo a month, ravaging it. During the period of these incursions the terror inspired by the Company made every castle in the neighbourhood surrender. Crowds of mercenaries who had finished their term of service flocked to Moriale, hearing exaggerated rumours of the great spoil gained by the Company, and many soldiers refused all engagements, saying that they would serve under this freebooter only."

Moriale observed the greatest exactitude in the distribution of the booty. Objects that had been stolen were sold by his orders, and he gave free passes to purchasers, so that by this means men who had been plundered might come to the fair he held and recover by payment the goods of which they had been despoiled. He instituted a treasurer, and had regular accounts kept of what was taken, and what prices were paid for things sold. He exacted as strict obedience as any feudal lord. He administered justice, and his judgments were invariably executed.

It was not till long after the English domination had ceased, and which had furnished these ruffians with an excuse for their violence, that the plague of the Free Companies was put down. One of the very worst of all was that of the "Ecorcheurs," or Flayers, and had nothing whatever to do with the English. It was headed by Alexander de Bourbon, a mere boy, who had been given minor orders to enable him to hold a fat canonry. The Flayers professed "that all the horrors hitherto committed from the beginning of the war would be but as child's play compared to their exploits."

A great Council of Captains of Companies was held at Monde, in the Gevaudan, in 1435, when the soil of France, of Aquitaine, of Languedoc, of Provence was parcellec up among them, each having his region allotted him in which to plunder and work havoc.

So long as the English held Aquitaine it was impossible for the crown of France to control this terrible plague. Every baron, every little noble, as well as every great prince who found his liberty in the least touched, his misdeeds reproved, at once transferred his allegiance to the English crown, and the English king was too far off, and too greatly in need of assistance, to be nice in choosing his partisans, and not to wink at their misdoings.

The money that had been taken from Levi was restored by Jean del' Peyra, but not without murmurs from those who had assisted in the capture of l'Église Guillem. The peasants could see the justice in surrendering every article recovered to the claimants who could establish their rights and show that they had been plundered of these objects. Even the book of the Chanson de Geste of Guerin de Montglane had found an owner. Most of the ecclesiastical goods had been restored to churches. Articles of clothing had been divided among those who had helped to take and destroy the vulture's nest. This all seemed to them reasonable enough, but that so large a sum as a hundred livres should be surrendered to a dog of a Jew, solely because he had been despoiled of it—that was what they could not understand. If he had been robbed of the money it was well—Jews were made to be plundered. Equal justice was not due to those who had crucified the Christ. Jean, had however, been firm, and had held to his intention. Rather than irritate the peasants to rebellion against his decision, he surrendered to them his entire share in the spoil of the robber's stronghold.

The gratitude of the Jew at the unexpected recovery of his money was profuse. Jean paid little regard to his demonstration. A year later and he had reason to congratulate himself on having done an act of justice, for Levi assisted him in the purchase of the Seigneurie of Les Eyzies with it feudal stronghold and the flourishing village at its feet. But this is an event of the future. We are concerned now only with what took place in the memorable winter that saw the destruction of the band of Le Gros Guillem, and that preceded the great battle of Castillon and the ruin of the English cause in Guyenne.

Jean had become exceedingly anxious to obtain tidings of Noemi. After the terrible death of her father, the butchering of his followers, the surrender of Domme, and the dispersion of the remainder of his band, he knew not what had become of her. She had relatives at La Roque—the Tardes—that he knew, and he was therefore satisfied that she was not homeless anc destitute. But that anything out of the wreck of Le Gros Guillem's accumulations had been preserved for her, he was doubtful. Who Guillem was, whence sprung, of what parents, no one knew. Whether he had any surname no one could say. Like many another Captain of the period he had escaped from the common mass of adventurers by the force of his abilities, by his superior power, by his daring courage. It had been so with that redoubted soldier of fortune, "Le petit Meschin,"[6] who from a scullion had risen to be the scourge of whole provinces, and to defeat and well-nigh exterminate a royal army under a prince of the blood. Even renegade priests had headed bands of brigands and distinguished themselves by their outrages of all laws human and divine.

[6] "Picciolo servo fuggito, di oscura lugo nato."—Villani.

The "Église Guillem" in the rocks of the left bank of the Vézère was no inheritance of the robber chief, but had been taken by him and occupied as a stronghold of his own, and none had dared to reclaim it and attempt to dislodge him, till the attack by the peasants that has been recorded.

Jean felt that a painful obligation lay on him to see Noémi. Her father had met with a terrible death at the hands of his father, who had played with the wretched man as a cat with a mouse before he had cut the cord and precipitated him to his death. Le Gros Guillem had forfeited every right to command sympathy by his treatment of Ogier—in casting him down the oubliette and then by his treacherous attempt to have him murdered by his two men-at-arms. Nevertheless, he was Noémi's father, and his mangled corpse lay between Jean and her, and across that and the terrible wrongs committed by the dead man and the revengeful execution the hands of Jean and Noémi could never meet.

But the word of affiance had been spoken, and spoken solemnly, before many witnesses, and it had been sealed with the giving of a ring. Such a word could not be broken. In popular superstition it bound even beyond the grave. Release could be had only by mutual consent and the restoration of the pledge. Jean rode to La Roque, full of trouble at heart. He loved Noémi, he greatly esteemed her. He saw in her a noble soul struggling to its birth with aspirations after something better than what she had known— gladly would he have taken her to be his, and helped this uncertain, restless, eager spirit to unfold its wings, to break out of its shell, to look up and to soar into a pure atmosphere—but it might not be. The terrible shadow of Le Gros Guillem, the awful story of the past made this impossible.

As he was nearing La Roque, he suddenly drew rein—he saw Noémi. She was seated on a mass of brown fallen leaves, and was plucking helebore flowers. Even that act struck Jean to the heart. "She plays with poison—seeks out the noxious, the deadly," he said. He leaped to the ground, and holding the rein of his horse came to her.

"Noémi, what are you doing?"

"I am making a chaplet for the grave of my father."

"Of helebore?"

"What else suits? Would you have it of the innocent flower of the field? On such he trampled. They call this the wolf's flower—enfin! It is a flower!"

"Noémi, do you know why I have come?"

She stood up, holding the half-finished wreath in her hands and looking down. She did not answer, tears filled her eyes and trickled over her cheeks.

"Noémi," said he gravely, "you recall that incident by the charcoal-burner's lodge, that moment of terrible danger when the peasants, mad with revenge and success and the blood of the wolves they had killed, would have torn you—"

She did not answer. As she raised her hand with the helebore wreath, he saw that the ring was on her finger where he had placed it.

"I said what I did then, and I placed on your finger that ring, which is indeed your own—as you had entrusted it to me to show to your father—and I declared before all present that you were affianced to me. It was so."

She bowed her head.

"But, Noémi, you know that this can never, never be."

She looked up quickly, sadly at him. Her eyes were full of tears.

Jean was deeply agitated.

"You must return me the ring—if only for the form's sake, so as to undo the pledge and dissolve the engagement—I will give it back to you as a surrender of a loan—as nothing else."

She put her fingers to the ring and drew it off, and without a word offered it to him.

He took the ring and looked at it, doubtful what more to say.

"Noémi," he asked, "whose arms are these engraved on it? They seem to me to belong to the Fénelon family."

"Yes—they are the Fénelon arms."

"Was the ring—" He was about to ask if it had been stolen, but checked himself.

"It was my father's ring," she said in a low tone.

"Your father's! Was Le Gros Guillem a Fénelon?"

"Le Gros Guillem! Oh, no! Do you not know and understand?"

"Know, understand what?"

"Le Gros Guillem was not really my father; he carried off my mother from Fénelon, along with me when I was an infant in arms. Le Gros Guillem killed my father, who was the Baron de Fénelon. But I was a child and I was brought up at Domme. I knew nothing of that. Le Gros Guillem always treated me as his child and loved me as such, and I—I always called him and looked up to him as father."

"Noémi—is this true?"

She gazed at him full in the face. "I am no liar, Jean."

"Noémi, throw aside that helebore, open your arms. To my heart! to my heart! Take back the ring, all is well, is well. Mine for ever!"

## CHAPTER XXVI

THE ELEVENTH CROSS

Ogier Del' Peyra had returned to Le Peuch Ste. Soure. His appearance greatly astonished the people, as his beard and moustachio had been shaved, and his hair, usually worn very thick and long, had been clipped close. So transformed was he in appearance that they could hardly recognise him. It was not till the story of the exploit of La Roque had reached them in its entirety that this transformation was understood.

Ogier would say nothing about what he had done. He relapsed into indifference and silence, and appeared morose and inaccessible. He took no interest in anything connected with his lands, none whatever in the great political events that ensued.

On September 20th, 1452, John Talbot, Earl of Shrewsbury, disembarked on the coast of Medoc and entered Bordeaux on the 22d. Several small towns and fortresses surrendered. Then a large French army descended into Guyenne. On July 14th, 1453, the main body, under the command of the Count of Penthièvre and the Admiral Jean de Bueil, encamped at La Mothe-Montravel, and prepared to lay siege to Castillon that was held by the English. Talbot at once quitted Bordeaux, accompanied by between eight hundred and a thousand horsemen, and followed by from four to five thousand foot soldiers. He arrived before Castillon on the 17th of July.

At the approach of the English the French withdrew to their camp, and were followed by Talbot, who arrived breathless, his troops exhausted with a long march. Misinformed as to their numbers, believing that the French were retreating in alarm, without waiting to recruit his troops, the Earl of Shrewsbury resolved on storming the French camp.

The mistake was fatal. Not only did the French army vastly outnumber his own, not only was it fresh, whilst his troops were fagged, but their camp was well chosen and well defended with artillery that played upon the English from every side with disastrous effect. The defeat was complete. Talbot and his gallant son fell, and their death has been immortalised by Shakespeare. Nor has the great dramatist failed to point out the cause of the failure—the disunion among the English leaders.

This memorable battle prepared the way for the final deliverance of Guyenne and of France, not from English arms only, but from the plague of the Free Companies, which had grown and spread under the shadow of the English domination. At length the south—which as yet had not been in name even French—was absorbed into the kingdom, and partook of the benefits of union, and began to tingle with the lifeblood of the nation.

Ogier del' Peyra resigned all concern relative to his estates into the hands of his son, or rather the management was taken from him by Jean, because the old man could or would attend to nothing himself. Whether his mind had been affected by his imprisonment in the oubliette, or whether the inactivity was constitutional, and when the necessity for exertion and the motive for revenge were passed he could no longer rouse himself to action, remained uncertain. He had expressed no surprise when Jean brought Noémi to Le Peuch as its mistress. He accepted whatever happened as a matter of course.

For long he did absolutely nothing but sit in the sun and bite pieces of twig and straw. If addressed, he replied only with a "Yes" or "No," and gave tokens of annoyance if anyone was persistent in forcing a conversation. Whether he was thinking of the past, or thinking of nothing at all, none could say. Most certainly he gave no thought to the future, for he made no provision for the morrow and left everything to Jean.

At last he became feeble, and when feeble suddenly took it into his head to absent himself for a good part of the day.

On inquiry, Jean learned that he crossed the river taking with him a hammer and chisel; and he was informed that the old man had been seen scrambling up the slope to the ruins of l'Église Guillem. One day, accordingly, Jean went after him, and on reaching the cave-habitation found his father seated on the floor engaged in chipping with his tools.

"What are you doing, father?" asked Jean.

The old man did not answer with words, but pointed to the floor. He had been trimming into shapeliness the crosses that marked the lives taken at the storming of l'Église.

"But there are eleven, father," said Jean, pointing to one larger than the rest, fresh cut.

The old man nodded. "For Le Gros Guillem," he said. "I killed him."


Sabine Baring-Gould – A Concise Bibliography

Sabine Baring-Gould's full bibliography consists of over 1200 works.  Many of these are songs and hymns with the best known being 'Onward Christian Soldiers'.

A Book of the Pyrenees (1907)
Court Royal (1891)
A Book of Dartmoor (1900)
A Book of North Wales (1903)
A Book of Ghosts (1904)
A Book of South Wales (1905)
A Book of the Rhine from Cleve to Mainz (1906)
A Book of The West: Being An Introduction To Devon and Cornwall (2 Volumes, 1899)
A First Series of Village Preaching for a Year
A Garland of Country Songs (with Henry Fleetwood Sheppard) (1895)
A Second Series of Village Preaching for a Year
An Old English Home and its Dependencies, London, 1898
Arminell
Bladys of the Stewponey (1919)
Cliff Castles and Cave Dwellings of Europe
Cornish Characters (1909)
Curiosities of Olden Times (1896)
Curious Myths of the Middle Ages (1866)

Dartmoor Idylls (1896)
Devon (1907) (Methuen's Little Guide on Devonshire)
Devon Characters and Strange Events (1908)
Domitia (1898)
English Fold Songs for Schools (1907)
Eve
Family Names and their story (1910)
Grettir the Outlaw: a story of Iceland (1890)
Iceland, Its Scenes and Its Sagas
In the Roar of the Sea (1891)
In Troubadour Land: A Ramble in Provence and Languedoc (1890)
John Herring
Lives of the Saints, in sixteen volumes (1897)
Legends of the Patriarchs and Prophets (from the fall of the angels to the death of Solomon).
Mehalah, A Story of the Salt Marshes (1880)
Noemi
Old Country Life (1889)
Pabo, The Priest (1899)
Red Spider (1887)
Sermons on the Seven Last words
Sermons to Children
Songs & Ballads of the West (in 4 Volumes 1881-1891)
Songs of the West: Folksongs of Devon & Cornwall (1905)
The Book of Were-Wolves, being an account of a terrible superstition (1865)
The Broom-Squire (1896)
The Gaverocks
The Life of Napoleon Bonaparte (1908)
The Lives of the Saints – a sixteen-volume collection (1872 and 1877)
The Mystery of Suffering
The Pennycomequicks
The Preacher's Pocket
The Tragedy of the Caesars (1892)
The Village Pulpit (1886)
The Vicar of Morwenstow, being a life of Robert Stephen Hawker (1876)
Urith
Village Preaching for Saints' Days

www.ingramcontent.com/pod-product-compliance
Lightning Source LLC
Chambersburg PA
CBHW071326130626
46556CB00004B/1767